The Michael Chronicles

Book 1

April Boden

Contents

For The A team, I love you.

And for the spellers, you are the TRUE experts.

Praise for the Michael Chronicles: Book 1

April Boden's introductory novel skillfully brings you into a word that will expand critical thinking while simultaneously experiencing the range of emotions She writes with an uncommon sensitivity and vividness that draws you into an adventure into a beautiful life expanding a world view of how to overcome obstacles, process emotions and how to make life-changing decisions. A must read! - Jean-Marie Finn, mom

Set in the 90's where technology didn't monopolize our lives, and music still had soul. This takes me back to the days of the Goonies. I'm excited that the Michael Chronicles embodies that spirit for today's children. Children need a story like this to strengthen their spirt, and ignite their imagination. Can't wait for the sequel. - Virstyne Henry, author co-founder of Truther Talk

I love, love, love this book! The charismatic main characters take us with them on a ride that is exciting, dangerous, and entertaining. The story

unfolds through the eyes of Michael, a nonverbal teen, thus providing the reader insight into the intelligence, empathy and bravery locked within many who cannot express themselves verbally and does so in a way no scientific or medical journal could. I cannot wait for the next chronicle with Michael and the guys. – Roberta J. Anderson, business owner, grandmother of non-speaker

Told through the eyes of a teenage boy who does not speak but uses a letter-board to spell, this wonderfully crafted story, set delightfully within the 90's era, makes an entertaining mystery reminiscent of your favorite movies of the past. Get to know Michael and see what the world looks like through his eyes as he helps his family when they need help the most! This is a book you won't want to put down! - Meadow Davidson, co-author, blogger, and mother of neurodivergent children

Chapter 1

THE BIG MOVE

The morning we left our San Francisco apartment for Jukeville, Colorado, I was a bundle of nerves. I've always been rather intuitive, so maybe I had an inkling of the irrevocable changes for better or worse that our family was facing. The empty walls and floors of our small 2-bedroom caused me to ponder the unknown. In the summer of 1992, I'd never been to the new place or even a different state. My life experience up to this point was limited and nothing about me screamed or even whispered that I'd be the type of person to have adventures. Most wouldn't peg me as being able to do much of anything, not in a mean way, it's simply they don't know any better.

My fingers flickered within a half an inch of my face, intermittently flapping by my sides as I paced through the empty space, following my family closely wherever they went, the bathroom, the truck, the kitchen where Mom pulled out those remaining chopsticks left resting isolated in the utensil drawer.

"Michael, you need to stay clear," Mom said, gently pushing me back, out of her space, then handing me a heavy box of pots and pans.

For the remainder of the day, she had me carry boxes, plants, small appliances and basically anything she thought heavy enough to ground me but not so fragile, I might break it. I followed her lead as we loaded the rented trailer attached to Mom's minivan. Between the trailer, the minivan, and Dad's small Datsun 210, there was only so much we could bring, so a lot of our stuff lay abandoned on the sidewalk of Sacramento Street with a sign stating, 'free stuff'.

Mom couldn't wait to escape the city she grew up in to carry out her dream of living in a small town. She drove Dad's car that day, even though she hated driving it normally, but she didn't want the hassle of driving the van with the hitch. My little sister, Alyssa and I rode in the back while Mom kept a bag of healthy snacks in the passenger seat, tossing over the occasional apple chip, water bottle or meat stick. Dad's radio was broken, but Mom had a portable boombox that she kept in the front, popping in a mixed tape she'd made recording songs off the radio. Once Laura Branigan's "Gloria" came on, Mom bopped around, singing each word. This was her song, at least to me. Her name isn't Gloria, it's Bridgett, but it reminded me of her on the exercise bike and sounded like busyness or people walking fast. I could envision her scuttling through the kitchen closing a cereal box and putting it away before lifting a fork off the floor with her toes, rinsing it in the sink, closing the cabinet door above her head and without so much as a breath moving on to the next task.

I must say, I miss those afternoons we used to have once our school day was over, seeing her in the kitchen race to the radio and hit record to the song she wanted. When she cleaned, she listened on her Walkman waiting for those phone in contests where you're the 10th caller and win a thousand bucks or a trip to Disneyland. She never won, but as soon as she heard the cue, she'd race to the phone and dial. If it was busy, she'd hang up and press redial over and over until the disc jockey came back and announced the winner. She wouldn't give up, no matter how many times she failed. I never understood why she wanted to wear headphones instead of playing it on the boombox. Perhaps she didn't realize I could hear everything anyway, headphones or not.

Rustling around with boredom, Alyssa scanned through her copy of Disney Adventures, while I noticed the tear in the vinyl on the back of the passenger seat. Tapping on it as it dangled there, then seeking to remove it by peeling the piece back, revealing the cushion underneath.

"Hey Mom, Michael is ripping the seat." Alyssa said.

Mom glanced back at me. 'Oh no, busted,' I thought as I immediately stopped pulling back the piece and returned to tapping on it.

"Ugh, this car is falling apart. I can't wait to get out of here. What about you guys?" Mom said.

"Not really. Why do we have to leave again?" Alyssa asked.

"We've already been over this a dozen times, honey. Your Dad is a scientist and now finally has a chance to put his skills to work. No more retail or restaurant jobs. We have a house now: you'll have your own room. We all will." Mom said.

"Can I make it all princessy?" Alyssa asked.

"Well, I don't know. Who's your favorite princess?" Mom asked.

"Uhm... Cin... I mean Ariel." Alyssa said.

"Were you going to say Cinderella? You know she's my favorite princess." Mom said smiling as they played this game of 'Who's Favorite Princess' for the umpteenth time.

Alyssa roaring with laughter, started to climb her way into the front seat.

"Hey, hey, you can't climb up here. Stay in the back." Mom said.

"But Mommm... I want to be with you." Alyssa said with a tinge of a whine to her voice.

I knew even when Alyssa was a baby that she was special. She is the only person I've ever met who carries a pink glow. It's like at her soul's core she's partially made of bubble gum. Before we found out about Dad's new job, Alyssa had her 8th birthday party at the ice-skating rink near the beach where she used to take lessons. I always loved the shocking icy feeling I'd get the minute I walked into that place. My big brother, Ethan headed straight through the saloon style doors to the lounge area, ordered a hot chocolate and posted up at the Galaga, where he'd always hit the top score, beating his previous score each time.

Mom bustled around, delivering the plates, drinks, and cakes to the birthday room. Alyssa's cake was specially made with an ice skater on the front. I couldn't eat any of it, but Mom used the flour blend she created with only soaked and sprouted grains to make a cake for me.

Not the greatest skater, Dad skidded on the ice twisting his ankle, nearly busting it while Alyssa trotted on and off the rink, showing her friends her new mittens. Noticing the stop and go game on the wall, a relic from before arcade games, costing only a nickel, I went to it. The glow of green and red lights with the shimmer of silver from the trim drew me in as I tapped on it, flicking my fingers in my face with the anticipation of their blinking.

Alyssa and a couple of her friends sauntered by as one of the girls, wearing a purple tutu and pigtails, stopped to observe me, "Ehh, what's wrong with that boy?"

"Whoa, he's so weird," said the other.

"No, he isn't weird." Alyssa said.

"He's like retarded or something." The first girl continued.

"No, you're retarded. He's smart!" Alyssa said giving the girl a little push on the shoulder.

Stunned, the two girls walked away as my belly filled with bubbles and aches, causing me to unexpectedly laugh.

"You, okay?" Alyssa asked brushing her hand on my back.

Without skipping a beat, I continued tapping on the stop and go, while Alyssa skipped over to the mini arcade posting up next to Ethan on Ms. Pac-Man.

Meanwhile, on the road, Mom continued driving well into the night. While Alyssa fell asleep on my shoulder, I remained wide awake. The blackness of the Utah sky was enveloping. There was nothing except the reflectors on the road and the billions of stars I'd never seen on any San Francisco night.

Nearly 12 hours on the road, with little stopping, we finally pulled into a motel. Dad and Ethan were already there, waiting outside the minivan with keys in hand.

"Hey, hun, we're in room 112," Dad said as he kissed Mom.

"Good, I'm exhausted, you?" She asked.

"Of course," Dad said with a sigh, placing his arm on her shoulder.

Ethan came to the car and picked up Alyssa carrying her to the room. It smelled of ammonia and looked like one of those roadside motels you'd see in a movie with velvet paintings and coin-operated beds. Exhausted, we all plopped on the bed without so much as turning on the TV and headed to sleep.

The next morning, I was awakened by Mom pulling my covers off and forcing me into the shower. Alyssa was bouncing around the bed, blasting morning cartoons while Ethan jibbed her, pulling her down on the bed, tickling as she squealed with laughter. Dad walked in with coffee and donuts in hand.

"What? Donuts? We can't eat that." Mom said.

"Sorry, this is all I could find. Where do you think we are?" Dad asked.

Rolling her eyes and turning back to me in the shower, Mom handed me a washcloth, instructing me to wash my face, armpits, then backside.

I'd never eaten a donut before. I found it crazy sweet and within minutes; I felt jittery. My stomach filled with creepy crawlies that tickled from the inside. My laughter was uncontrollable as I dwelled on one of the velvet paintings, rubbing the raised smooth texture. There was a matador in a blue suit, standing erect as his red flag warded off the mighty bull. The gold trim on his blue suit glowed and swirled, while cascading like a river. It was so incredibly beautiful I tapped on it, believing it might feel wet, but it wasn't, it was smooth like the rest of the painting.

"Michael, knock it off," Ethan said.

Stopping, I noticed the motel room was empty, and the family was waiting in the car except for Ethan. Taking my shirt at the shoulder, he yanked me out of the room, directing me to the Datsun where Dad stood in the doorway on the driver's side talking closely with Mom.

"Hey bud, you get too much sugar in that donut?" Dad asked with a smile, tapping my shoulder.

Giggling, I began following him to the minivan as Mom called me over to return to the Datsun.

After about 6 hours on the road, I was starving. I tried feeding thoughts into Alyssa's head telling her I was hungry. I also needed to use the bathroom. I focused heavily on the ripped vinyl in front of me, flapping to distract myself. To my chagrin, I could see through my peripheral Alyssa was sleeping; so much for getting into her head.

Mom pulled into a truck stop diner. Laughing and flicking my fingers in my face, I couldn't contain my relief.

"Excited, bud? I bet you're hungry. Me too." Mom said.

Racing to the entrance, I flung the door open, then realized no one was with me. Flicking my fingers in my face again, I could hardly hold my bladder, but couldn't figure out how to get to the bathroom.

Several people sitting in the waiting room looked up at me with a combination of confusion and fear. An elderly woman leaned over to the man next to her, whispering with eyes on me, while a little girl clutched her mother's skirt. Flinging open the door, Mom swiftly approached with a slight smile and an apologetic face. Squeezing her arm tight, she tried to console me.

"It's okay honey, we're going to the bathroom now," she said.

As Mom dragged me to the woman's restroom, I had to go so bad, I hardly noticed the peering eyes melting through my skin. The open door revealed 3 stalls and 7 or so people waiting. Taking hold of Mom, I dug my chin into her forearm; she tried to calm me. Slight movement happened as one stall opened and another and another but still with 4 people in front of us, I paced back and forth running to the sink washing my hands, then watching the slow drip of water off my fingers. Mom called me back to the line, standing next to her I could hold it no more. A sudden calm came over me as I looked Mom deep in the face, wishing I could tell her how sorry I was as the pee rolled down my leg.

Chapter 2

GOOD OL' COLORADO STEAKHOUSE

In late August, Alyssa and Ethan were getting ready to head back to school. Mom and Alyssa went into town to shop for school clothes while Ethan stayed home with me. Dad started work right away and despite his long days at the lab, plus helping us set up the new house on the weekends, he was loaded with energy.

"I'm telling you, we're working on cutting-edge stuff; it's bound to revolutionize medicine." He'd say.

Dad must be a genius, I thought. I couldn't wait to hear more about what he was doing. Over the weekend, Mom and Dad set up the basement for my homeschooling.

"This is perfect, John," Mom said, throwing her arms around Dad's neck.

"Yeah, it's gonna be good for you and Michael," he said.

"No, not just good, it's great. I can finally do this the way I imagined." Mom said, looking around at the setup complete with ABC charts, a chalkboard and one of those circle time carpets even though it was only me to sit on it. I liked the texture of the chalk and couldn't help but to always pick it up and start tapping on it. It's hard and soft at the same time; grainy like tiny shells mashed together.

When everyone was out, that's where Ethan and I spent most of our time.

He listened to records while working on his art. Back then, he never let anybody see his art, which made me feel special. It was based off the characters he created playing Dungeons and Dragons; I liked the wizards most. He'd always play his favorite band, Rush. The moment Mom left; he'd crank up the volume to 11. It hurt my ears sometimes, but I liked the music. Neil Peart's drumming was ferocious but controlled. I could see laser like streamers shoot up into space each time he slammed his stick down onto the drum. I can't say I care for all prog rock, but Rush is friggin' awesome. I knew all the words and sang along, but what came out of my mouth was different than what it sounded like in my head as Ethan always told me to be quiet. In my head, it was perfect.

Once "Freewill" from Rush's second album "Permanent Wave" came on Ethan got to tapping his pencil on his notebook, singing in a low whisper under his breath.

It was the song that most reminded me of him, probably because he listened so often but maybe there was something in the lyrics that reminded me of Ethan's quiet bravery. I loved that Dad made sure to put the old record player in the basement. It was always my favorite part of the day when Mom played it. It felt like our time: our only time that wasn't a bustle, a rush, or a worry. Though her lips sang tunes, her face and smile spoke joy.

When Alyssa returned from school, she would ask, "Why don't you play these with me, mama?" As she held the records up, waving them around in Mom's face.

Mom busily continued making dinner and tending the chores, so Alyssa opted to dance with me.

"Five little monkeys jumping on the bed," she sang, holding my hands swinging my arms around. This caused me to love that music, despite myself.

The sound of Mom pulling up the driveway rushed me back to the present as Ethan turned off the turntable and we made our way upstairs.

Mom kicked the door open, huffing her way over to the dining room table, plopping two full bags of groceries down. Trailing behind, Alyssa slowly sauntered in, swinging two small plastic bags and wearing a new pink hat.

"What's with the hat?" Ethan asked.

"It's new. I got it for school." Alyssa said.

"You're never gonna wear it," he said, swiping it from her head.

"Stop, I will wear it," Alyssa said, reaching for it as Ethan played keep away. "Mom, make him stop."

"Could you please? I need help, there's more groceries in the car." Mom said as Ethan gave Alyssa her hat back, then headed for the door.

"Take Michael; there're groceries for the whole week," Mom said, stopping Ethan as he gestured for me to come on.

The door to the minivan was wide open, revealing 3 full bags of groceries. Ethan took one and handed it to me, then proceeded to grab the other two as I followed him back into the house.

"On the counter," Ethan said while gesturing to where he wanted me to place the bag.

"Did you get anything any of us are going to like, or is it all 'Michael' friendly?" Ethan asked.

With her head in the refrigerator, Mom continued, "Yes, it's good for you and tastes great, if that's what you mean."

"Awesome," Ethan said in a sardonic tone. "What's for dinner tonight, anyway?"

"Tacos." Mom said.

"Now we're talking." Ethan said, pulling out a bag of grapes shoving several in his mouth.

"Food is either medicine," Mom started as she began cooking dinner.

"Or poison, I know," Ethan said, throwing a few more grapes in his mouth, "maybe Dad will take me out for some poison later."

"Don't count on it. There's no fast food in this town." Mom said.

"I saw a pizza place earlier," Ethan said.

Jukeville was in stark contrast to our previous city life. The downtown area was a cutesy historic relic of the old bustling mining town that no longer existed. The outskirts were full of dilapidated buildings, junkyards, and miles of mountains. Something in between was what you might call a neighborhood. Sure, there was a hospital, schools, a fire department, and all that, but it was so sparse compared to the stacked on top of each other environment I was used to. I hadn't seen where Dad worked yet, but he said, 'It was restoring the town's economy.'

"Can you turn on the radio?" Mom asked Ethan.

"Mom, no radio; I want to watch TV," Alyssa called out from inside the living room.

"Here's your Walkman," Ethan said, handing it to Mom.

Hearing the rattle of Dad's old Datsun 210 pulling up the driveway, I hovered around the front door, anticipating his entrance. His grassy green glow emanated as he put his finger over his mouth, giving me the 'quiet' sign so he could sneak up behind Mom, surprising her with the flowers he was hiding behind his back.

"Ahh, John, why did you sneak up on me like that?" Mom said with a start.

Dad planted a kiss on her cheek, and she smiled at the sight of the flowers, pulling her headphones down. Running into the kitchen, Alyssa wrapped her arms around Dad's legs. He reached for her, picking her up and spinning her around.

"Where's the big one?" Dad asked.

"Basement." Alyssa said.

"Are you guys going out tonight?" Mom asked.

"We all are. Let's go to dinner in town. I heard about a great steakhouse," Dad said.

"I'm already making dinner." Mom said as she continued stirring the meat and vegetables in the skillet.

"Save it. That's what Tupperware and refrigerators are for. We'll have it tomorrow. Or you and Michael can have it for lunch, whatever, let's get outta here, woman," he said, smacking her on the behind.

"Ahh, fine," Mom said with a giggle as she turned off the stove.

"Go get Ethan; tell him to get dressed, and no t-shirts; it's gotta be at least a collared shirt." Dad instructed Alyssa as she excitedly raced downstairs to the basement.

About an hour later, we found ourselves sitting on oversized red vinyl couches impatiently waiting for a table at Coral's Good Ol' Steakhouse. Overwhelmed by the smell of grilled steak, I leapt out of my seat, flicking the straw I had lifted off the bar when Mom took me to the bathroom. The décor was old western, like a scene from that show Dad used to watch, Bonanza. The walls were decorated with mounted dead animals, paintings of John Wayne, Ronald Reagan, and other cowboy types without an inch to spare.

Finally, the hostess ushered us to a table next to the fireplace. The warmth of the fire was attractive and simultaneously a little intimidating. Mesmerized, I found myself repeatedly trying in vain to blow it out, which had my parents giggling for some reason. Then Dad's gaze turned to a couple of men heading towards the door.

"I'm thinking medium rare ribeye for me and Michael with salads, no croutons, water, or maybe they have juice. I don't see it on the menu," Mom said, realizing Dad wasn't paying attention. "Hey who are you looking at?"

"Oh, I think that's a guy from work." Dad said, subtly gesturing to the men with a tip of his head.

One man stood holding the door for the other, gently guiding him forward as the other looked down at the straw. He held in his hand, flicking it the same way I was a minute ago.

"Oh, should we go say 'hello'?" Mom asked.

"Nah, they're leaving, and it looks like the waitress is coming. I'm starved." Dad said, looking back at his menu, wrapping his arm around Mom with a smile.

Chapter 3

NOT JUST ANY OTHER DAY

As the months went on in our new town, it started to feel like home and not some foreign planet we were vacationing on.

Christmas here was a trip! Such a stark difference from San Fran with the bustling streets and department stores stacked with folks ceiling to floor. Each year we'd go to the Emporium to visit Santa and there'd be at least 100 kids every night waiting, sitting on the floor or bouncing off the walls, heaving great sighs of boredom through each scene of the city carefully crafted with Legos. Don't get me wrong: it was a cool display, but the waiting was unbearable. Either Mom or Dad would have to take me outside and walk me around. The best night was the time it rained. The streets glistened while the fresh scent of water overpowered the usual car exhaust. Dad held my hand as I tapped my foot in a huge puddle reflecting the green and red lights, surrounded by yellow tape.

I have nice memories of those Christmases, but in Jukeville it was like a Hallmark card come to life. The downtown was tastefully decorated with subtle draping of evergreen garland wrapped with red bows and adorned with white lights. Each night of December leading up to the day, there were carolers walking the streets and even knocking on doors like in *Oliver Twist* but without the figgy pudding. Mom dragged us out almost nightly as she gushed over the 'quaintness', taking copious numbers of photos. And the snow! At first it was like our own amusement park while Alyssa giddily made snow-people who she pretended were real giving them full *Days of Our Lives*, soap opera story lines complete with snowman love triangles and other such betrayals of life in Snowapolis as she called it. By Christmas, it turned from being magical to somewhat of a drag.

Initially, San Francisco still felt like home. At night hearing the symphony of crickets, I'd miss the constant clank of metal, moving always, from the Wharf to the Cliff House, overlooking the ocean giving the atmosphere its misty air, which lent credence to the feeling of a place past its prime. I'd dream of that park in Chinatown where Mom took me during the day to swing and could almost smell the mixture of farts and fried dumplings. The steam perpetually rising through each crate, manhole, then softened by the wet rolling fog. I dreamed of it until one day; I didn't and Jukeville became home.

Once Mom took Ethan and Alyssa to school, we'd drive into a nearby town, bigger than Jukeville, but still not big enough to be called a city. They had a grocery store Mom liked, Country Life Harvest, which carried all the ingredients she needed. It reminded me of the stores in San Francisco where you could buy anything from candles to cabbage all in one store only for a much higher price than a normal store.

"Oh, look, its organic strawberries on sale, so late in the season, I wonder where they are from," Mom said, darting to the bin of strawberries, carefully examining them before choosing the ones she placed in the cart.

"Hey there Mrs. Hogan. The usual?" The young man behind the counter at the juice bar called out.

"Yes, David, I think we will." Mom said, walking towards the bar as David held out two paper to-go cups with a large coffee for Mom and a pumpkin smoothie for me.

As Mom reached out to hand me my smoothie, I snatched a pencil sitting on top of the counter, causing a stack of papers to fall to the floor.

"What's this?" Mom asked, lifting the papers off the floor.

"Oh, that? A newsletter I'm reading, conspiracy stuff," David said.

"Conspiracy, like aliens and three-headed dogs?" Mom asked.

"No, nothing like that, like creepy experiments and stuff. You can keep it." David said.

"Oh no, that's okay," Mom said as she reached to hand it back to him.

"No, seriously it's yours. I think you'll find it, enlightening." David said.

"Alright," Mom said with a smirk as she threw it in the cart, and we continued our shopping.

After we got home, I helped Mom carry the groceries inside while she started unloading the items and placing them in the fridge.

"What's this? Oh yeah, it's that conspiracy rag." She said, shoving the newsletter David gave her in a drawer.

Mom got busy cooking second breakfast. The aroma of sizzling bacon had me hovering. In the morning before Ethan and Alyssa went to school, we'd have first breakfast which was something like fruit, yogurt, or cereal. Second breakfast was much heartier with a nice warm bacon or sausage, pancake, eggs, potatoes, and the like.

After we ate, we headed to the basement for our school day. Mom had drawn a bunch of words on the chalkboard with the letters in dotted lines like you find in those kindergarten books. She took my hand and had me trace, D-O-G, C-A-T, B-O-Y and so on. Growing fatigued with the lesson, I took the chalk in my hand and started tapping.

"Hey Michael, come over here. We're not finished." Mom said.

Slowly, I headed back to her, tapping the chalk the whole way. Once again, she took my hand and lead it to the board where I started to trace, D-A-D, then I remembered some chocolates she picked up from the store earlier today, which she hid in the cupboard above the stove. Going rogue, I stopped tracing the words Mom had written as I really wanted to say, 'Hey, can I get some of those chocolates?'

"What are you doing?" Mom asked. "Do you want to draw or something? Not feeling the words today, huh?"

No such luck for spelling on the chalkboard, so I dashed over to the alphabet board and started tapping on it.

"Oh, you like that alphabet board, don't you?" Mom asked.

I wanted to say, 'No, not really, I just want to tell you something,' but oh well, I knew where the chocolates were and could sneak out of my room at night and snatch them.

"Alright, let's switch it up." Mom said, gliding across the room to put "I Eat Apples and Bananas" on the turntable.

Blurting out a giggle, I made my way to her, still tapping chalk. I could see a big smile on her face as she danced with outreached arms. The squeeze of her hand caused the chalk to press into me in a way that I enjoyed. As she held my hands, swaying me back and forth, her smile ushered in a much brighter blue glow than normal, which peered through each pore of her skin and streamed through each focal of hair. This always happened when we danced.

It wasn't bad schooling with Mom; it was merely beneath my intellect. To be fair, it was even less so at typical school. I liked it when she read to me, which she did an awful lot. This was the only time she gave me age-appropriate material. One day, we were at the art store, and I made a beeline to this stack of chapter books. I always wanted to read the classics. There was *The Jungle Book, The Call of the Wild, The Wizard of Oz* and *Wind in the Willows,* held together with a blue ribbon. Picking up the books, I held them by the ribbon. Mom thought maybe I liked the satin texture of it, and I did, but truthfully, I wanted the books. It was only five dollars for the set. Mom looked at me and for a minute, it felt like she had figured it out. It would take much longer for her to truly get it, but at least she bought me the books.

The day in question was not extraordinary in any way, nor was there any previous indicator that things were about to change so drastically. Except for maybe Dad had been a little different. No-one but me appeared to notice, but his grassy green glow was dimmer than normal the past few months. Other than that, I can't say there was any way to predict what was about to happen. Alyssa and Ethan came home from school as normal, while Mom took to the kitchen preparing dinner.

When Dad came home from work, he headed downstairs to talk to Ethan. He did this most nights and perhaps it deserves mentioning that they were best friends. Dad was jittery like he'd had too much caffeine and decided to take Ethan to the park to kick around the soccer ball. Ethan hadn't been on a soccer team since elementary and he wasn't that into it anymore, but he didn't have the heart to tell Dad. He loved him so much.

It was after dark, and they had not returned for supper. Alyssa and I ate without them, but Mom couldn't sit still. She kept going into the kitchen, taking out this or that. She'd put the potatoes on the table, sit down, then realize she forgot the butter, so she'd have to get up and go back into the kitchen. This went on all through dinner. It wasn't that unusual for them to be late, so I wasn't sure why Mom was acting this w ay.

Finally, Dad and Ethan came through the door. Dad was limping and had his arm around Ethan for support. Mom rushed to him and helped Dad to the couch.

"What happened?" Mom asked, but before he could answer, she said, "I knew something was wrong, I just knew it."

"It's fine." Dad said. "Just a sprain."

Ethan ran into the kitchen and brought some frozen peas. Mom insisted since he watched Alyssa and me so often that he became certified in First Aid. He knew what to do.

"You need RICE, Rest, Ice, Compression, and Elevation" Ethan said.

He ran to his room and grabbed his first aid kit, taking a tube of Neosporin, some iodine, and a wrap. Dad had great difficulty taking off his shoes and socks. When he did, we saw his foot and ankle were horribly disfigured, like they were trying to bend the wrong way; sitting there mangled and bleeding, unable to move. Mom gasped and Alyssa screamed, running into her room, carrying-on the whole way, then running back to watch as Mom took a warm wet cloth to clean the wound. Ethan treated and wrapped it, then reapplied the frozen peas.

Despite the chaos, Mom had us go through our nightly routine. She took me and Alyssa to the bathroom, had us potty and brush our teeth, read us a story, then put us to bed. Ethan stayed up with Dad until Mom told him to go to bed, too. I couldn't sleep while listening to Mom and Dad talking through the walls.

"It doesn't look good, John," Mom said. "I'll have Ethan watch the kids for a little while and take you to the ER, it's not a big deal."

"That's right, it isn't a big deal, so let it go." Dad said.

"What about nerve damage, John?" She asked.

Mom was probably referring to his diabetes, which Dad had as long as I can remember, though he didn't look like someone with the ailment.

They chatted for a bit longer before things finally got quiet.

I lay awake thinking how strange their conversation was. Mom hated hospitals more than anything. She thought that most modern medicines were meant to 'make you sicker', but Dad was a scientist who believed that medicine held the keys to miracle cures. It was odd that he was the one refusing to go to the hospital.

Around 2 in the morning, while wandering my room in the dark, I heard a screech, sounding like Dad, but in such a way I had never heard before. Mom jumped out of bed and started to get dressed.

"You're GOING to the hospital," she said in no uncertain terms.

She went into Ethan's room and instructed him to watch us. Ethan got up and helped her walk Dad to the car. Walking out of my room, I stood in the hallway flapping my hands while pacing.

When Ethan saw me, he told me to "go back to bed." I went, but I didn't sleep that night.

That was the last time I saw Dad.

Chapter 4

THE HOSPITAL

The following morning, I knew Mom was back when I heard the shuffling of feet, shifting of utensils, and clanking of pans coming from the kitchen. She was making waffles with her special all-purpose flour blend.

The thick, sweet concoction of flour, eggs and milk slowly poured on the waffle iron, making that sizzling sound as the steam rose. Though normally I was perpetually hungry, it was hard to eat with my stomach tied in knots, worrying about Dad. When Alyssa and Ethan walked into the room, Mom insisted we eat as we sat with urgent faces.

Turning around, plate in hand, she said, "everything is fine. It's good we caught it early as it may have grown infected, which would have complicated things a bit, but it was a good break. Not so clean, a bit mangled, and he's having his surgery this morning. Ethan, can you take your sister to school? I need to be here when the hospital calls."

"Sure, Mom," Ethan said.

The time dragged, while Mom scanned the radio, settling on "Simple Man" by Lynyrd Skynyrd, which she used to sing to me as a baby. I knew this because whenever it played, she'd say 'I used to rock you to sleep with this,'

She buzzed around, wiping counters, seats, doorknobs, and anything else she could find, then started cleaning out the refrigerator. It might appear odd that Mom, and the whole family for that matter, were nervous since it was only a broken foot, but I think it was because Mom always said, 'People go into the hospital with one problem and come out with 3 new ones.' That . . . Or because we sensed there was something she wasn't telling us.

When the phone rang, Mom was in the middle of cleaning out the refrigerator. Juggling 3 items in her hands, trying to figure out where to put them, she screeched, "AAARRRGH," The ketchup, bag of spinach and cauliflower went flying to the floor as she raced to pick up the phone.

I could hear a woman's voice on the other end say something about 'insurance'.

Mom responded, "No . . . I mean, yes, of course we have insurance. It's through his employer. I'm sure this is a misunderstanding; I'll be down in a bit."

She hung up and turned to the shards of glass and splattered condiment on the kitchen floor. Gingerly tiptoeing through the maze with bare feet while mopping up the mess.

"Okay, no class today. We need to go to the hospital and get Dad. That's a certain type of education, I guess, huh? You think? Alright, let's get dressed." She said.

Spotting a straw resting on top of my dresser, I headed into my room and began bopping it as I waited for Mom.

"Grab a shirt," she said, pointing to the top drawer where they were kept; then I opened the drawer below it, pulling out a pair of pants.

Frozen, I waited for her to pick out my clothes, rather than face the rejection of receiving pants once again, when I wanted a shirt.

You can't imagine how frustrating it is to know where your shirts are, which are your favorites, and not be able to grab one on command.

The therapist that used to come had me work on this 'skill' ad nauseum, laughably speaking in a monotone voice stating, 'GET SHIRT'. So silly.

This led a lot of people to think that I didn't understand what a 'shirt' was, or know the difference between shirts and pants. I mean, give me a break. The ridiculous ideas some people get.

When I was 3 years old, Mom took me to one of many assessments I had over the years. A man in a suit with glasses, holding a clipboard, presumably a doctor or PhD or some 'expert' along those lines, told her, "He doesn't understand the difference between a living thing or an object."

"No, that can't be. He is so sweet." Mom said.

"Of course, you want to believe that we all do, but the harsh reality is that you are no more important to him than the toothbrush he's tapping on." He said.

Then, lunging forward, I flipped the table and bit him in the forearm. We never saw that 'expert' again.

Mom handed me a shirt, which I proceeded to put on backwards. She pointed to my shoulder, giving my shirt a little tug, which I knew was my cue to turn it around.

After getting dressed, we took off in the minivan. An eerie feeling overwhelmed me as I fixated on Dad's beat-up old Datsun in the driveway.

Upon arriving at the hospital, I picked up a pen from off the floor of the car and ferociously began tapping. As Mom got out, I remained seated.

Opening the door, she said, "Come on, let's go."

As I got up, she held my hand while we walked in.

On the other side of the automated doors, I could see the sterile white floors and walls. The smell of ammonia and pine wafted over the sea of sick people in the lobby.

Mom marched up to the counter while the hive of nurses buzzing around continued to ignore us. She dinged the bell, getting the attention of one of them, pulling her away from a conversation.

"May I help you?" She asked.

Her name tag read 'Nurse Delores.'

"Yes, my husband was admitted last night." Mom said.

"What's his name?" The nurse asked.

"John Hogan" Mom said.

The nurse looked at her clipboard of papers and scrolled through each. She was puzzled, as if she couldn't find it.

"Can't you find him? Try Johnathan." Mom continued.

"What was he admitted for?" The nurse asked.

"Just a broken foot!" Mom said.

"Why was he admitted overnight for a broken foot?" The nurse asked.

"Isn't it your job to know those questions? I don't know . . . he needed a surgery . . . they said it needed to be done right away, and he had to stay. Is there a manager or someone around here who knows what's going on?" Mom said.

Nurse Delores' brow furrowed as the blood drained from her face. Without a word, she went behind a closed door, where I could hear her whispering to a male voice. After about 10 minutes of tapping my pen like nobody's business, Nurse Delores came out from behind the closed door with a man, presumably the one she was talking to. He was tall, brown hair, brown eyes, clean cut, nice looking and with the darkest, ugliest brown glow I had ever seen. Grabbing Mom by the arm, I began digging my chin into it.

She looked at me and said, "it's okay, Michael, we won't be long."

I stopped for a minute, then began again, while making the sound, 'waah . . . waah. . . waah . . .' Mom did her best to ignore me and addressed the man with the brown glow.

"Hello Mrs. Hogan, let's step over here, shall we?" He said.

He wore a suit, not scrubs or a white coat and no name tag. We stepped aside to a small corner of the room where there was a fish tank. The bubbles floated up and out of the filter, like when I was young, and Dad took me to the park with an 80-cent pink bottle of bubble juice. He lifted me on the swing as I reached for each clear, sparkly ball. Using a finger, nose and even his tongue, he'd pop each one, causing the rainbow to drip wet on my bare legs. It was a nice distraction. If I didn't have something else to focus my attention, I most definitely would have started to meltdown.

"Mrs. Hogan, we had a complication," said Dr. Brown Glow.

"I knew it. Can you guys do anything without screwing it up? I mean, it's just a broken foot. Can't you set a break? You have to do more; you have to mess with people." Mom ranted.

Dr. Brown Glow touched her arm, getting her attention, causing her to stop. For a moment they were both silent, then as Mom looked at him, she began to shake, putting her hand to her mouth as if she already knew what he was about to say.

"Mrs. Hogan, there was a complication during surgery and I'm afraid we couldn't save him," said Dr. Brown Glow.

"What?" Mom asked, then paused, turning white, then red. "WHAT? What are you talking about? That's impossible. It was a broken foot! People don't die of a broken foot; they don't come to the hospital for a routine surgery and DIE, What's wrong with you people?"

She cried, then keeled over.

Things around me turned into a fuzzy haze. The hospital looked like a Monet, No, more like one enormous cloud. Mom didn't notice me until I started to laugh. She came over and took my hand, while hugging me as I hugged her back, digging my chin into her shoulder. 'Waah, waah, waah . . .' I can't say what happened next. Everything went black, and the darkness is the last I remember.

Chapter 5

THE NEXT FEW MONTHS

The next few months felt endless. We all couldn't wait for each day to end. I either slept for several hours straight or not at all. It was maddening, and the storm was building. I am ashamed to admit but sometimes I grabbed or punched Mom and Ethan. Scared, Alyssa ran to her room and hid under the bed. I don't understand why I am not always able to control it. It's like when you leave the lid on a boiling pot, eventually the scalding water seeps out and overflows. My family usually thinks I'm hungry or uncomfortable, which can be a trigger, but I don't know, it's never that simple. All at once I feel everything, the pounding of my head, the cramping of my stomach, the tiny needles infested in my skin, the fatigue of my eyes and the heartache of being trapped. So, I grab, hit, bite, push or punch, followed by temporary relief, then an overwhelming sense of shame. It's a sucky cycle.

Certainly, these months have been bad for all, and I know I wasn't making it easier. I never cried and at Dad's wake, I laughed. People think this means I don't understand, or even worse, that I'm cold-hearted, but it's not that at all. I loved Dad more than anything. I missed him and couldn't believe he was gone. It's not me who responds 'inappropriately', it's my body. I am merely a puppet, my body the puppeteer. At best, it's entertaining.

People came in and out of the house all day, bringing us food. Mom didn't cook anymore. She let us eat whatever people brought. It was incredible to try things Mom would have never let me try before. For the first time since I was 3 years old, I ate pizza, tuna noodle casserole, spaghetti and meatballs, garlic bread. I mean, garlic bread! Mom never allowed bread unless she made it herself. Her bread did not taste like this. It was delicious and exciting to try new foods, but still; I missed Mom's cooking. Though some of it tasted amazing, it often left me with stomach aches which Mom attributed to why I was being more aggressive. There might be something to that, though I feel my emotions often get ignored.

Nevertheless, I was prone to stomach pain. When I was 3 years old; I'd get a taste of a chicken nugget and in 10 seconds, my eyes would dilate, and I'd be on the floor lining up my books. My hands would swell like two balloons. To let the air out, I'd smack and press them into the floor, furniture, toys or whatever would give me release. Sometimes I felt like I had crossed over into another dimension where the walls were melting, and lights carried tiny glowing balls of color that floated away one by one. Mom's attempts to get my attention would result in my hysterical laughter. Unable to stop, I was convinced a tiny troll with the slenderest fingers and toes lived within my belly, wreaking havoc for his own amusement. As the years went on, Mom put me on medications and restricted diets, which turned the head trip to stomach cramps. When they became excruciating, I'd press my stomach into the ottoman for relief. If demands were put on me while

I was in this state, I'd bite, punch, grab . . . whatever I could to escape my own skin. The 'experts' told Mom to drug me and that it was my 'behaviors'. It's not too sensitive to assume its behaviors and the drugs only made me sicker. In this situation, you learn quick to suck it up and build better tolerance for pain.

After a couple of months of eating and grieving, Alyssa and Ethan went back to school. Ethan didn't want to stay home at all, but Mom made him. He kept going around telling everyone that it was "okay, we weren't that close."

I wondered if he was lying because it made the sting a little less harsh. Alyssa was crying all the time and slept in Mom's room. I got sick at one point and slept in Mom's bed too, feeling safer that way.

My birthday came and went. I enjoy getting balloons and presents, but I can only open one or two at a time, so Alyssa and Ethan open the rest for me. I'm not trying to be ungrateful for my gifts. I appreciate the thought, though I can't say I'm much into 'stuff'. This birthday was pretty good because we stayed home and one of our neighbors made me a cake. I swear I've never had 'real' cake before. Don't get me wrong, Mom's cakes are amazing, and I love them, but this was a whole new experience. Mom got me a new ball. I always got a ball for my birthday, Christmas, Easter, Arbor Day... It was better than a toy truck or car, I guess. I received a gift from Ethan this year for the first time, which was super cool. It said it was from Alyssa and Ethan, but I knew Ethan was doing yard work for neighbors and making his own money. It was a RUSH t-shirt! That was probably the coolest thing anyone ever gave me.

The card read 'because I know you like to rock.' Can you believe that? Ethan understood me more than anyone.

We didn't always get along. When I was little, I had these behavioral therapists that came to the house. Instead of preschool or sitting around watching cartoons like most kids, I had 30 hours a week of therapy. The first therapist brought in a suitcase full of toys and I liked her, though I remember struggling to stay awake after, say, the third straight hour. She had this animal puzzle that when you put the correct animal in the correct slot; it made a sound. The bear made a 'roar' and the chicken made a 'cluck', that kind of thing. My therapist, Melissa, held the pieces out and waited for me to call them by name. Eventually, I learned how to say, 'bear, duck, chicken' and all the other animal names. I had a few other words too and thought maybe my words were coming back to me, but they didn't. I don't know why, but one day, it all stopped again.

At that time, I started going to a special preschool in addition to the therapy I was receiving at home, and it sucked. I remember one morning, Mom took me for a walk in the park before class. It was calming, and I felt safe close to Mom. When she brought me to school, it was like a betrayal. I stood at the gate, banging my head with my hand, crying repeatedly, 'want Mommy, want Mommy.' But the teacher thought it sounded like gibberish. I think Mom understood and I could see her eyes welling with tears, but she left me at school, a nyway.

Adding to the difficulty, because of my new school schedule, Melissa was no longer my therapist and someone else came. I don't remember much about this new person, only that her glow was orange. I didn't like much during these days. My head felt like it was filled with gasoline, and someone lit a match; I banged it in an attempt to stop it from feeling so weird. I'd use whatever I could, toys, someone's arm, the wall. I've been known to leave holes in walls with this technique. Ethan was a frequent target of the grabbing, biting, and pinching. At first, he screamed and cried for Mom, but eventually, he fought back. As we got older, the fights were less frequent, but more intense. Mom intervened and usually got mad at Ethan, stating that he knew it was 'only making things worse.' Despite the fighting, I still thought Ethan was the best brother in the world. I still do. He gets me.

Celebrating my birthday wasn't half bad, but it didn't make things any less strange.

Alyssa fought tooth and nail to not go back to school. She only wanted to be with Mom, but Ethan couldn't wait. With the two of them gone, Mom slept a lot and sometimes sat on the couch watching soaps. This wasn't like her at all. She was always so busy and such a fighter. Grieving is odd, I'm not sure of the correct way to do it.

As weird as it was, things were about to get weirder, much weirder. One afternoon, a lawyer from the insurance company came to our house. Mom, still in her pajamas, invited him in. They sat on the couch as she brought him some coffee.

"First, I want to say I'm very sorry for your loss," said the insurance man. "This is the worst part of my job."

Then, pulling papers out of his briefcase, he continued, "I couldn't find your husband's policy, so unfortunately we can't award your claim."

Mom shook her head and for a minute, I could see the fight in her face return, as she spoke, "Excuse me, what? What do you mean you can't find his policy? I have three children and a mortgage. You better look again."

"I'm very sorry, but it just isn't there. His policy was terminated about 4 months before his death. I wish there was something I could do, but there's nothing." The insurance man said.

"Wait a minute, wait a minute, this is through his medical insurance, which was through his employer. Do you mean to tell me that not only do we receive no life insurance money but those hospital bills

I've been getting, thinking were a mistake are actual bills? Is that what you're telling me? How is this possible?" Mom asked.

"Ma'am, it appears your husband was terminated from his employment 4 months prior to his passing," he said.

"No, No, He was NOT. He went to work every day; he was the most honest man in the world. He would never lie to me or anyone else; this simply isn't possible." Mom demanded with urgency.

Then she kicked him out. As Mom started slamming the door, we spotted a stout fellow wearing a green flannel and jaundice yellow glow get into our minivan. Slamming the door closed, she shook her head, then flung it back open, sprinted to the man who was now sitting in the driver's seat with the engine on.

Throwing back the car door, she screeched, "Hey, what the hell are you doing?"

"Lady, you need to call the bank. I'm just doing my job," he said, driving off.

Mom huffed her way back into the house and started making phone calls while I thought about Dad.

What Mom said to the insurance guy was true; Dad prided himself on honesty. It's hard to imagine he was keeping secrets as they are inferring. I think part of why I was growing angry at this time, aside from the grief and the novel food, was like all these suits and whitecoats were trying to paint a picture of Dad that wasn't true.

The most baffling part was that we still didn't know what happened to him. I mean, there was never a clear explanation. He went in for a broken foot, had a routine out-patient surgery and died. They divulged he had an unknown heart condition, due possibly to having been a smoker many years ago, exasperated by the diabetes, and he had a heart attack during surgery. They further suggested he was a ticking time bomb that would likely have suffered a heart attack, anyway.

Now, I don't know much about deceit. When people contradict themselves, I usually give them the benefit of the doubt. I've never told a fib and don't even know what that feels like, but in this case, I was convinced everyone was lying.

Chapter 6

THE BIG BUILDING

After losing our minivan, discovering Dad had no life insurance, no medical insurance, and no job before he died, Mom woke up from her slumber and went into high gear. A lot of people, like her friends and Grandma, were trying to convince her that maybe Dad had a second life and wasn't who we thought he was, but Mom and I knew better. Something was up and Mom wanted answers. This was more of the Mom I recognized.

She showed me how formidable she could be when I was 6 years old. She had had enough of the behavioral therapist coming to the house and wanted better for me. She took me to these 'Centers' where a lot of psychologists, neurologists and other bureaucrats sat around one side of a large table and Mom and I on the other side. Most people would be intimidated, Mom wasn't.

She showed up with a large notebook and in it were chronicles from lectures she attended or photocopies from these monster textbooks she read. My heart was racing, and my knee was bouncing like mad, so Mom took my toothbrush from her purse and gave it to me for bopping. The 'experts' all tried to appear interested in me. 'Michael, you've grown so much.' They'd say with plastic smiles and their brown glows. Many of them, by the way, had never seen me before. I kept my distance.

The head psychologist began the meeting, "Thank you for coming in today and bringing Michael. We understand you're interested in funding a play-based therapy instead of behavioral therapy. We understand your concern; unfortunately, at this time we are only interested in evidence-based methods."

Mom pulled one of the pages from her notebook. "Interesting that you should mention 'evidence-based' when I have right here 'evidence' of this method being quite successful in early intervention."

One of the other doctors started in, "that's what's called 'emerging evidence,' we're looking for more established methods."

Mom responded, "Can you show me the 'evidence' that behavioral therapies have any successful long-term results?"

Then a third doctor chimed in, "at this time we're still in the phase of gathering long-term data."

"So, no, you don't have long-term studies? Is that right?" Mom said.

"It's the most evidence-based method at this time. Other methods have potential, but we can't fund those. You're welcome to find alternative forms of funding." Said the head psychologists.

This went on for a while, when the head psychologist said, "at this time your son is phasing out of early intervention, we find that there's a window of opportunity between ages 2-6, he will likely remain where he is for the rest of his life and the best that can be done is to mitigate behaviors."

By this time, Mom was losing her cool. Her voice became elevated as she said, "funny thing, this window of opportunity, I've searched and searched for any data on this, can you show me the data that such a 'window' exists?"

"It's based on," started the head psych.

"Is the scientific method merely 'based on' or does it require actual trials and study? I think you should know the answers to these questions since you're dealing with people's actual lives here," Mom said.

"I know you're frustrated but..." Head Psych said.

"He's miserable. You're making him miserable." Mom said, with hands flailing, accidentally knocking over a coffee.

Gathering her papers back into her notebook and taking my hand, she stated, "Clearly, I'm getting nowhere; you are not people of science; you hide behind your degrees; but if I were you, I'd go back to the university and ask for a refund, as it appears you were gypped."

That was the end of the meeting.

After getting back to the car, helping me with my seatbelt, then sitting in the driver's seat, she screamed as loud as she could while slamming her hands on the steering wheel. My body trembled, reaching for something to fidget, settling on the seatbelt flap. Mom began crying, which unnerved me.

After she composed herself, she turned around and spoke. "You deserve better. You deserve everything. Don't listen to them say that you can't or that there's some friggin' window that stops you. I've never heard of a window that doesn't open. If it takes a friggin' rock to open it, it still opens. Do you understand?"

I understood her, but I had my doubts that I'd ever be able to find a way out of my silent prison. When you hear people say things about you over and over, it becomes your identity. You can't speak for yourself, so others speak for you. They may have good intentions but get it wrong, you have no choice but to go with it. You start to forget what you wanted in the first place and finally stop having your own opinions; waiting for others to tell you what you want, like or think. My parents told me not to let that in and to fight it.

"Experts are full of shit. More often than not, you understand me?" Mom said. "I wouldn't trust them to screw in a lightbulb, let alone make decisions that affect the lives of complex individuals like yourself. You don't own it, not for a minute. They don't know you and they have no 'expertise' that gives them the right to decide your fate. We decide our fate. You know?"

She shook her head, wiped the remaining tears from her face, while turning around.

"Remember Wilma Rudolph," she said as we drove away.

Wilma Rudolph was a 3-time Olympic gold medalist in track. As a child, due to an illness, she was unable to walk and required braces on her legs. I too had braces when I was younger to stop me from toe walking. When asked how she did it, Wilma said:

My doctor told me I would never walk again. My mother told me I would. I believed my mother.

I memorized that quote because Mom kept it on the refrigerator and even when we moved; she brought it with us. I wanted to believe Mom; I wanted it so much, but sometimes I wondered if she believed it and that contradiction made me doubt.

"Let's go get some lunch," she said, smiling for the first time that day.

Her smile filled me with warmth, as I let out the air, smiling back; plus, I was starving.

Meanwhile, Mom was on the phone all week calling the hospital, the bank, and Dad's work to resolve problems and get answers. She told the hospital they'd have to wait for their payments, and they better not harass her about it. She told the bank the same, and they assured her under the circumstances they would not come to collect on the mortgage, though we'd have to drive Dad's old Datsun for a while.

Grandma insisted we come to live with her, but she lived in a condo and there wasn't much space. Besides, she was in California, and it would turn everything upside down for us kids again, or at least that's what Mom thought.

She called Dad's work to gather information about why he was terminated and for how long, exactly.

"What non-disclosure agreement?" Mom shouted over the phone.

"All employees are subject to an NDA, and it goes both ways." Said the voice on the other side.

"I was not aware of an NDA or whatever. I need to talk to someone that has answers. Can you put me on the phone with a competent person?" Mom said.

"Sorry ma'am, this is all I can tell you right now," said the other voice, right before it hung up.

Slamming the kitchen phone down on the receiver, Mom huffed. Pacing the floor several times biting her nails, she huffed some more, then called back.

"Hi, I believe we were disconnected. Where are the competent people in this building?" She asked.

Next thing I heard was the dial tone as Mom slammed the phoned, picked it up and slammed it back down three more times.

Whipping around to face me, she said, "Okay, Michael, let's get dressed. We're going over there."

None of us had been in the Datsun since Dad died. Looking for something to bop, I noticed a paper soda cup, which was empty except for the small remains of brownish liquid presumably melted ice infused with the remaining drops of Coke. Taking the straw out, I started to tap. Heading to Dad's work, I had the same feeling as when we went to the hospital.

Upon arrival, a long line of women in business clothes holding brief cases and notebooks snaked around the large grey building. In San Francisco, large buildings were common, but in this small town, it was an eyesore. Not that it was the prettiest area to begin with. The surroundings were nothing but dilapidated factories and abandoned junkyards.

Navigating past the long line of women; we found the main entrance locked. As someone opened the door to let the next woman in, Mom grabbed the handle and took hold of my shirt so that we could force our way through. The person who opened the door had her back turned, not noticing.

Mom headed to the receptionist sitting at a large, white, circular desk.

"Excuse me. Hey, excuse me." She repeated, growing louder.

On the phone, the receptionist, without even a glance, lifted her finger, indicating 'hold on'.

Looking over at me, Mom gave me a 'what the hell' face. Then a man in a suit, escorting the lady who had been let in the building before us, walked by. Staring him down, Mom caught eye contact as his face winced. Appearing trepidatious, he quickly escorted the woman out as Mom rushed towards him and I followed.

"Hello, do you remember me?" Mom asked the man.

His wrinkled light blue shirt, dark blue tie, and brown pants looked as tired as he did.

"Do you remember me?" Mom asked again.

"Yes, of course I do. I'm sorry for your loss." The Man said.

"I saw you at my husband's wake, the only person from his work who came." Mom said.

"Yes, we shared many assignments. He was a great colleague. I can't tell you how sorry I am," the man said.

"Can I talk to you a minute?" Mom asked.

"I'm in the middle of conducting interviews right now. As you can see, the recession isn't over yet," he said, exasperated.

"Please, no one will tell me anything. I don't know what to do," Mom pleaded.

He smiled at me, then standing in the open-door glancing at the long line of women, turned to Mom, "I can't. I wish I could right now, but maybe we could talk later."

Mom's eyes welling with tears, I could see the rejection and confusion was getting to her, when to my surprise she turned to the man and said, "I'm here for the job interview. I need a job." The man looked back at me when Mom said, "I will get a sitter once I can afford it."

He nodded as we walked back to his office.

He sat behind a messy desk. I could see papers were stacked high in a tray way too small for the number it was holding. A name plate on the desk read 'Dr. Cody McDougal' also several degrees on the wall read the same. It didn't look like the office of a scientist. In fact, I didn't imagine scientists to be in offices at all. I thought they were in labs looking through microscopes with long white smocks and safety glasses.

Sitting in a chair directly across from him, Mom gestured for me to sit in the chair next to her, but the thought of sitting still wasn't an appealing one in that moment, so I wandered over to the side of Dr. Cody's desk.

Mom gestured again and said, "Over here, Michael."

Still not feeling it, I grabbed a pen off Dr. Cody's desk that was resting on a large stack of papers held together by a silver fastener. I started tapping the pen when I noticed the cover of pages read: **CRO REPORT: AuthentaGLOBIN's clandestine trials.**

Being an avid listener, I consider myself to have a pretty good vocabulary, but I had no idea what any of those words meant.

Unconcerned by my behavior, Dr. Cody asked, "Do you have a resume?"

"Not with me, but I can fax you one before the end of the day." Mom said.

"What is your office experience?" Dr. Cody said.

"I need to know why my husband was fired. I don't know anything, I don't even know for how long, I know nothing, NOTHING. Help me out, please," Mom said.

"We all sign NDAs when we come here," Dr. Cody said.

"Enough with that shit. I don't care about the NDA, my husband didn't sign an NDA, he would have told me. He didn't keep secrets. If you knew him, you would know that about him." Mom said.

I agreed with Mom. Dad would have said something.

"Mrs. Hogan, I really want to help you, but I don't know the details of John's termination." Dr. Cody said sympathetically.

"Well, you must know something. If you worked together, what were you working on right before?" Mom asked.

"Mrs. Hogan, I think the interview is over." He got up from his desk, gesturing for Mom to stand.

"Alright. I mean, look, you don't know what it's been like. My husband wasn't sick. None of this made sense, none of it makes sense. Can you sympathize at all? Do you have any compassion? I really do need a job. I have a mortgage, hospital bills and anyway... Yes, I am experienced. I have over 10 years working as an office manager and a paralegal. It's been a while. I mean, I quit to stay home and teach

Michael, but I have excellent references." Mom pleaded as Dr. Cody sat back down.

Putting his hand on his face, covering his mouth, he sat back in his chair and sighed deeply, then sat up, straightening his posture.

Looking at me while putting his face into his hands again, he asked, "You're Michael?"

"Yes, that's our Michael. I'm sorry I had to bring him. I will be signing him up for school. He should be able to start as early as Monday." Mom said.

This was the first I heard about starting back at school and I can't say I liked the sound of it. Alyssa was in elementary and Ethan in high school, which meant I'd be alone.

Grabbing Mom's arm, I started digging my chin into it. 'Waah, waah...'

Her face flushed, whispering to me, "please, calm down Michael, please calm down."

"Michael, you remind me of my younger brother," Dr. Cody said.

Stopping abruptly, I looked up at Dr. Cody.

"Mrs. Hogan, I can start you on Monday!" He announced.

Shaking her head with a start, Mom said, "Uhm, okay, I'll see you Monday."

Taking one of the cards from his desk, Dr. Cody wrote a series of numbers on the back.

"This is the code to get in the building," he said, handing it to her.

"You may not have noticed due to the crowd out front, but there's a number pad that everyone needs to enter a code into, to get in. You can bring your resume, driver's license, social and all that with you on Monday. What are your computer skills? Oh, never mind, don't answer that. That was a question to ask before I said, 'start on

Monday,' we'll just figure it out as we go. Sound good?" He stood up and reached his hand out to shake Mom's.

Straightening her blouse, Mom stood up and shook his hand while biting her lip, which was something she did when trying to fight back tears. "Thank you, Dr. McDougal, 9am?"

She looked like she wanted to say more, but that's all that she could muster in the moment. I don't know if she was excited about the job or relieved that someone finally showed some decency. Then Dr. Cody did something surprising that almost never happened. He put his hand out for me to shake also. I knew what he wanted me to do, but all I could manage was to smack it like I was trying to give a high five. A handshake was foreign, while a high five was something I knew. Dad taught me by playing this game, 'up high, on the side, down low.' If I got the down low hand he'd say, 'you're a pro,' if I missed, he'd say 'too slow.'

As Dr. Cody escorted us out of the building and we headed for the car, I could hear him inform the women in line that the job had been filled. Without turning around, I heard a big roar, then mumbling from the crowd, followed by moping, cursing, and pleading.

One woman went so far as to beg, "Please, I will work for free as a volunteer. Please..."

Hearing that, I realized how lucky we were that Dr. Cody hired Mom. If he hadn't, we probably would have moved into Grandma's condo and wouldn't have met Jarek. I might not have learned to spell, let alone the truth about Dad.

Chapter 7

BACK TO SCHOOL

After leaving Dr. Cody's office, Mom enrolled me in school. The minute we walked in, I picked up an abandoned broken pencil left on the floor near the entrance and started tapping. The desire to bolt was strong, though I knew we needed Mom to have this job. The people at the office handed her a packet and said I could start on Monday, but they'd have to set up an assessment with the school psychologist, the occupational therapist, the speech therapist, the physical therapist, and in 30 days they'd have an IEP (Individual Education Plan) meeting with Mom. Mom knew the drill.

Over the weekend, Mom and Alyssa headed to town to get Mom new clothes for work and school, while Ethan and I stayed home. Ethan stayed in his room, drawing and listening to Rush. I paced around outside his room, waiting for the door to open, but it never d id.

Sitting on my bed thinking about school and life amongst the normal made me fidgety. I raced to the couch, plopping down, rocking back and forth, then bouncing my knee, then dashing to sit on the toilet even when I didn't need to go. Barreling into Ethan's room, I bounded atop his bed, bopping my toothbrush, but he paid me no mind. It takes a lot of energy controlling my body when it has a mind of its own. I don't want to grab or punch people; I don't want to pour an entire bottle of mouthwash down the drain or eat toothpaste or break my sister's toys, but my body tells me what to do and I obey.

On Sunday night, Mom came into my room after we had been made to return to our normal bedtime routine. This included brushing teeth and hair, taking a bath, practicing a relaxing guided meditation (or at least Mom wanted it to be relaxing), and reading a story. Since Dad died, we had been falling asleep on our own, whenever and wherever we wanted. I preferred the routine. Mom came in holding *The Call of the Wild*. She picked up where we left off over 3 months ago. As she read Jack London's words, I contemplated the protagonist, Buck. What was he feeling, getting yanked from his comfortable home only to be forced into a life of hardship in the Alaskan wild? And though it wasn't what he wanted, he comes to appreciate it, to recognize his true nature and find freedom.

At the end of the chapter, Mom turned to me, giving a big hug. I held on super long and tight, thinking about how I'd miss her during the day while at school.

"Thank you." She said as I picked a few pieces of lint and a couple of loose strains of hair away from her sweater.

Giving me an Eskimo kiss, she smiled, stroking my head, "I love you so much. You are the sweetest, most loving person I have ever known. I am excited to start back at work because it's a new hope for us. I want us to be able to stay here in this house and build a life. I never wanted or expected it to be like this, without your Dad but this is how it is. I will miss you, spending time with you and being your teacher. I will stay on top of your school as best I can and make sure they're treating you well. I know things have been rough at schools in the past, but I have a good feeling it will be different this time. Can you be brave?"

I smiled back at her, blinking my eyes in an attempt to communicate that I would try to be brave for her. She kissed me on the forehead, hugged me one more time before turning off the light and going to bed.

Monday was a big day for all of us. Mom bounded with energy like I hadn't seen in months. She spent the weekend putting together her paperwork, preparing our lunches and dinners for the week, and trying on all her new clothes to see what outfits she wanted to put together. She even made time to get a haircut.

She said she was using credit, which she called 'fake money' and that it was an investment, but we'd have to 'tighten our belts' for a while.

I was more nervous than excited, though my ambivalence over returning to school was overshadowed by my desire to help my family. And family is everything.

In elementary school, I had an aide who put together a photo album of my family trying to teach me the ASL (American Sign Language) signs for 'sister, brother, mother and father'. During break time, I requested my family photo album over toys or Playdough or time in the squeeze machine, lingering on pictures of my brother and sister. Though I never spoke to any of the kids in my class nor they to me, I considered them my friends, but my best friends were and are my brother and sister. I hated starting fights with Ethan and scaring Alyssa. The last thing I ever wanted to do was push them away.

When Monday came, Mom had Ethan take Alyssa to school while she took me. Starting in the office, she had all the paperwork they asked her to fill out completed and ready to go. A lady with strong perfume and black polyester slacks, which went swoosh when she walked, escorted us to my classroom while Mom repeatedly rubbed my shoulder. Swoosh, swoosh went the slacks as the shoes chimed in, clickety clack to the bottom level at the end of the school near the exit. I could see a few other students already there. One was sitting on top of his desk, and another on the floor.

The only student in her seat was a girl, rocking back and forth, repeating "got get away, got get away, got get away…"

Not a great sign.

There was another boy in a wheelchair who had no control over his head. It simply dangled from his neck. I hoped it didn't hurt. I wanted to show Mom I was a trooper, so I took a seat right away. Her face lit up as she came over to kiss me on the forward and say goodbye. I could see her eyes welling with tears.

Mom left the classroom with the slacks lady; I could still hear them talking in the hallway. She told Mom that starting next week, I'd be riding the bus to school. I took the bus to school before and it wasn't bad. It meant I had to get up earlier, but I liked the long, slow drive.

After sitting in my seat for about 20 minutes, the bell went off, but no one moved. The teacher and all the students continued what they were doing for another 20 minutes, before three young women talking to each other and laughing came into the room.

The head teacher, Mrs. Boulden, had her name on the chalkboard, but she said it to me anyway. She smiled, and I noticed she was wearing the same black slacks as the woman in the office. Perhaps teachers get a discount at the Black Polyester Slacks With A Swoosh Sound store, I wouldn't know.

This would not be so bad, I thought. Sure, they'd probably talk to me like I was hard of hearing or 5 years old, but I wouldn't let that get to me. I was determined to make the most of it, despite the distressing sounds made by the rocking girl on the other side of the room. I wanted so much to make Mom proud and make life easier for her. I was going to use every ounce of energy I had to keep it together, so Mom wouldn't have to be called out of work and come get me.

One of the women came over and sat next to me. "Hi, I'm Rebecca," she said, then spelled it out using sign language, "R-E-B-E-C-C-A."

I enjoyed watching people use sign language with their dancing fingers and exaggerated faces. My pre- schoolteacher was fluent in sign and when she did our morning circle time, she prettily signed throughout the 'Welcome song'. I understood most of it, but when asked to do it, my fingers and hands had a hard time forming the shapes. If I learned one sign, I'd get stuck on it and use it for everything. When cultivating the sign for 'water', I'd make my version of a 'W' with my fingers, then tap my chin. The only problem is I did it when I was hungry, tired, or wanting of pretty much anything. Same happened when I learned 'more', 'help', 'yes' and so on.

Rebecca was a nice, pretty, young woman, 20 something, still in college. She wore two braids on either side of her head and had blue eyes, like Dad. The only thing that truly annoyed me about her was whenever she spoke, she'd say things normally and then repeat them slowly.

Sometimes when Mom was working with me, we'd be doing some kindergarten level thing, like tracing letters or coloring. She'd tell me, "I know this is beneath you and you understand more than this, but it's practice. We must get your body to catch up to your brain."

Mom always knew I was smarter than most people gave me credit for. She must have since she read me books like *The Call of the Wild*.

Rebecca headed over to a locked closet and opened it with a key she had hanging off her jeans belt loop. Pulling out a few toys, a game board, and some puzzles, she came back over to my desk, placing them on the floor next to me.

Looking at the stack, then back at me as if to ponder what she thought I might like, she said, "You look like a puzzle man."

By happenstance or mandate or decree of law, the puzzle she grabbed was the same zoo animal puzzle I had every day for years, from every teacher and therapist since pre-school and beyond. My stomach acid started boiling, moving up to my head and the tips of my fingers. I grabbed the ends of the table, as my body whispered in my ear, 'go ahead and flip it'. Feeling the weight of it, I looked at Rebecca, and could see she noticed the distress in my face.

Quickly she switched to a pegboard, saying, "Maybe not this puzzle, M-A-Y-B-E N-O-T."

Laughing out loud, I realized it was going to be a long day.

Chapter 8

JAREK

Rebecca sat outside with me while we waited for Ethan to pick me up from school. After rummaging through my lunchbox, she passed me a left-over box of cut fruit and a water bottle. Despite the rough start, I could see I was going to like her. She had a nice aquamarine glow and smiled a lot. She spoke slowly to me, which I found a little annoying, but her tone was nice, soft, almost whispering. I hoped she'd be with me every day.

Some schools didn't offer 1-1 aides, which drove Mom crazy. The worst was when she fought tooth and nail, only to get me a wretched one.

Spotting Ethan in the distance, approaching with a new friend, I started giggling and flicking my fingers in my face.

"I just love your smile and laugh. You have the sweetest dimple." Rebecca said.

"Are you Michael's brother?" She asked Ethan.

"Yes, I'm sorry I'm late," Ethan said.

"No need to explain. I received a call from the school. We always need to stay late for clean-up duty, so you just got me out of clean-up for the day." Rebecca said, smiling at Ethan, then back at me.

She gently took my arm to help me up while nudging me towards Ethan.

"I had fun with you today. F-U-N." She fingerspelled, then gave the sign for 'fun,' waved goodbye and was off.

"Alright, let's get a move on. We still have to pick up Alyssa." Ethan said.

Then I froze. If you'd ask me why I stood stiff, I couldn't tell you. All I know is my body, and I often work as two separate entities. Ethan yanked the sleeve of my hoodie, pulling it half off, then taking his backpack started smacking me from behind. Though he is two years older, I was as big as him and he couldn't move me, no matter how he tri ed.

"I can't take this. Come on you loser, let's go," Ethan said.

The funny thing was, I wanted to go with him. I wanted to please him, but something in me froze. This happened from time to time, and it was always in the worst moments.

To my surprise, Ethan's friend chimed in, "Hey man, I'm Jarek. Long day, huh?"

The stiff cement in my shoulders started to dissolve as I looked at him through the peripheral of my eye. I could see he glowed bright blue, almost purple.

Touching my shoulder, he addressed me again. "Hey man, we gotta pick up your sister. I know it's a drag to be rushed around and all, but you know how it is. We got detention. Can you believe that shit? Listen, I got five dollars in my pocket. Grandma gives me $5 a day for lunch, but guess what? I never buy lunch. She makes me a big ol' breakfast every morning and a big ol' dinner every night, so I skip lunch and save the money. By the end of the week, I have $25, which I spend on movies, records, comics, candy, whatever I want. Anyway, after we get your sister, I can take this $5 and we'll all go to the store, buy candy, soda, whatever you pick out, man, my treat. Does that so und alright?"

Loosening up, I began to walk with them.

"Alright, man, let's go!" Jarek continued with a big smile as we made our way to Alyssa's school.

When we arrived, Alyssa was furious, declaring, "I'm better off walking myself home. And I'm telling Mom."

Once she learned we'd be getting candy, she lightened up and by the time we got there; she forgot all about it. I picked my usual Sesame Honey Crunch.

"Why would you pick that?" Alyssa asked in a disapproving tone.

Mom had me on such a strict diet that for years I never ate store-bought candy. When she finally allowed me to have some, the only kind I ever got was the Sesame Honey Crunch. You know, the one that sits at the counter of every liquor or convenience store on planet Earth. I don't know why I didn't disobey Mom's wishes when I had the chance, but to tell you the truth; I like the Sesame Honey Crunch.

Finally home, Alyssa dashed to the TV.

"Ahh, man, you made me miss Tiny Toons." She groaned, grabbing a bag of chips, and settled onto the couch to watch TV.

Ethan motioned Jarek to follow him as they headed for the basement.

"I'm going downstairs!" He shouted to me and Alyssa.

"I don't care." Alyssa said.

Following them downstairs, Ethan put his hand out to stop me.

"I don't mind," Jarek said, shrugging his shoulders.

In the basement, Ethan pulled out "Moving Pictures" by Rush and set it on the turntable.

"Yeah, that's what I'm talking about," Jarek said while air-drumming to the music.

Turned out Rush was Jarek's favorite, as well. Then, to my surprise, Ethan opened his notebook, showing his art to Jarek.

"Ahh, man, this is good." Jarek said, flipping through the pages while sitting on the couch.

"Yeah, that's my Paladin, a little different than the one you were drawing." Ethan said.

"Totally, I can tell," Jarek said.

Looking at me, then back at Jarek, Ethan asked, "Hey, how did you do that?"

"Do What?" Jarek asked in return.

"You know, get Michael to come with us today. How do you know about that stuff?" Ethan asked.

"I don't really, I mean, sort of... My Grandpa, he's uhm... Well, I don't really know what you call it, but he doesn't talk either. When I first got here, he was fine, you know, he's military too, just like my parents were." He pointed at his himself, then continued, "I'm a military brat. Anyway, he went to get a check-up, physical or something, you know, whatever it is they do. Then he came home, got sick for a few days, then had a stroke and that was it. He doesn't talk, he gets mad about stuff, and so I just learned how to talk to him to calm him down. I don't know. I figured he's still the same person on the inside. He just can't do stuff like he used to."

"Whoa, that's so weird. I mean, it's sort of like what happened to Dad. He went into the hospital for a broken foot..." Ethan said.

"I thought you said he had a heart attack?" Jarek said.

"He did. Or that's what they said," Ethan said.

"You don't believe them?" Jarek asked.

"Of course, I do. My mom doesn't." Ethan said.

"Man, don't even get me started. I was about four, maybe five years old and Moms took me to this Town Hall Meeting when we were living in South Central. There was this white man, retired LAPD or something, but also used to be in the CIA or FBI. One of those. He swore in front of everybody that the drugs that destroyed our community were brought in by the CIA. Everybody in the room went crazy." Jarek said.

"Whoa, that's a messed-up story, but what does that have to do with my dad?" Ethan asked.

"It's just to say that messed-up people do messed-up shit. That's all. They do all kinds of shit." Jarek said.

"Who are 'they'?" Ethan asked.

"I dunno," Jarek said with a shrug.

"Oh shit. My mom is here." Ethan said, noting the sound of Mom entering the house, then turning the music off before bolting upstairs.

Mom dropped her purse, briefcase, and keys on the dining room table while Alyssa dashed over, attacking her with a hug.

"Oh, thank you sweetie." Mom said, hugging Alyssa back. "How did it go today?"

"Good," Alyssa said, then glaring over at Ethan, Jarek and me coming into the room, she continued, "Ethan was 2 hours late."

"What? 2 hours late? Ethan, why 2 hours late? Can't I count on you?" Mom asked.

"Mom, it wasn't my fault. I had detention," Ethan said.

"Detention? Well, this story keeps getting better," Mom said.

"It wasn't my fault. I was late for school because I had to drop off Alyssa, then when I tried to have the school call you, I didn't have your work number. So, I had them call Michael's school at least to tell them I was going to be late." Ethan said.

"Oh geez. I'm sorry to all of you." Mom said, to our surprise. "It isn't fair to make you pick up all your siblings."

Now, looking down at Alyssa and stroking her hair, Mom continued, "How about I sign you up for the AM/PM club?"

"Yes, yes, yes, you're the best Mom ever. All my friends go there and it's so boring here." Alyssa said.

Looking back at Ethan, Mom said, "You'll still need to pick her up, but it will buy you some time until 5pm, okay?"

With a groan and a shrug, Ethan rolled his eyes, looking down at the floor.

Putting her hands on his shoulder, Mom said, "I'm sorry honey, I'll call the school tomorrow and make sure they know the situation and make sure you have my number."

"Hello, who are you?" Mom asked, noticing Jarek.

"Oh me? Nobody. I mean, my name is Jarek. Don't worry, I've seen it all. All kinds of family stuff, it's no big deal." Jarek said.

"Uhm. Okay." Mom said.

"We met at detention, but don't worry, I'm a good kid. I didn't get detention for any good reason, either." Jarek said.

"Oh no, what did you get detention for?" Mom asked.

"I don't even know. Being black." Jarek shrugged.

"Oh. You're right, that's not a good reason. You're welcome to stay for dinner." Mom said.

"No, thank you Mrs. Hogan, Grandma needs me home for dinner." Jarek said, as he headed towards the door.

"Good night," he said to Mom, and then looked back at Ethan. "See you tomorrow."

At the time, it all felt so normal.

Chapter 9

THE RECORD STORE

The first week of school, Mom woke up early so she could take Alyssa to the AM/PM Club. The PM part of the club closed at 5pm, so Ethan and I needed to do that part, as Mom's work ended at 6pm.

Mom said she didn't know how she was going to pay for it as she was only making $8 an hour and it was barely enough for our mortgage. By now, people stopped bringing us food too.

At school, I mostly did whatever Rebecca said and followed her lead. She'd tell me to go to the bathroom, I would. If she said it was time for snack, I'd eat. If she pulled out a puzzle or game for us to play, I'd do it. I was biding time until Ethan came to get me afterschool.

I was supposed to be taking the school bus, but they needed to put in the paperwork, and this took a few weeks. In the meantime, Mom dropped me and Alyssa off while Ethan walked himself in the morning, picking me up on the way home in the afternoon.

My school ended at 2:30pm, Ethan's ended at 3pm. Rebecca and I waited outside while I ate one of my leftover snacks. Rebecca was exceptionally understanding when Mom explained the situation about Dad and everything.

Jarek was with Ethan everyday now.

One Friday afternoon, for the first time in my life, we went to the record store. The second Ethan opened the door, earsplitting heavy rock rifts whooshed over me in an aggressive gust, which might have been too loud, sending me into a tailspin were it not for years of being desensitized by Ethan's blasting Rush. I felt mesmerized by the raucous sound and raw energy pulsating like a cut on your hand, hot and beating. The funky bass resonated in my joints, delivering a soothing pressure. Everything from my cheeks, nose and hair follicles vibrated. I had never heard the song before, but I later learned it was The Red-Hot Chili Peppers rendition of "Higher Ground", definitely one for the mixed tape.

A tall skinny kid with headphones leaned half his butt on a table tapping a pencil and before I knew it, my body took me there, as I fixated on the colored lines flicking from his pencil. My fingers flicked back and forth as I lunged my head closer to the pencil, the music still pounding through me.

"Hey Michael, over here," Ethan called out as I redirected my attention, following his lead.

The place might have been too much, if not for the fact I was captivated. Every inch of the walls was covered with posters of bands and album art. Jarek noticed a couple of guys from their school as he tapped Ethan, then gestured towards the two guys.

Ethan nodded to the guys, muttering, "S'up."

Following Ethan and Jarek past 1000s of records and tapes labeled, 'Electronic', 'SKA', 'New Wave', 'Punk', 'Reggae', 'Rap', 'Hip-hop', then when we got to 'Grunge', Jarek stopped and turned to Ethan.

"This is what I wanted to show you," he said, pulling out an album.

While the title was obscured, the cover was red, with a bundle of hands reaching up. Drunk from the dizzying sensory bonanza, I wandered over to a poster on the wall. It was painted black with a red rose that floated off the page in 3-dimensions. Trying to touch the lines, I tapped on them as they appeared before me like the steam coming off a fajita plate in a Mexican restaurant.

"Let me show you something, man," Jarek said while guiding me over to a glass booth.

It reminded me of a place Mom took me years ago, to get my hearing tested, when they thought I might be deaf. Boy, were they wrong!

Escorting me inside the booth, Jarek said, "You can listen here instead of buying it and waiting to listen at home. I do this all the time. We're not made of money, right?"

Jarek reached around to grab an LP single resting atop a stack of records siting on a barstool outside the booth. The cover looked like a textbook with a green jacket and gold trim. It read 'New Order: Ceremony: In a Lonely Place Fac.33'.

"It's a Joy Division song even though it says New Order." Jarek said. "The singer died, and this was his last song, but recordings were so bad, they had to replace it with a new singer and changed the name of the band. I think you'll like it."

He put the record on the turntable and walked out of the booth as I followed.

"Nah, man, you stay here and listen. We're right over there," he said, gesturing to where Ethan was standing, combing through records, then shut the door behind him.

Flapping my hands, I could see Jarek walk over to where Ethan was as they started talking, though I couldn't hear what they were saying.

Once the music began, I forgot all about being uncomfortable that I was in there alone. It was another song I had never heard before.

The lilting sound washed over me, then through me, lifting me off the ground as the gold trim reverberated like a guitar string. It waved and then stretched out to the ceiling. As a low melodic voice came in, I slowly descended effortlessly, landing my feet on the ground.

My body swayed while musical notes floated off the record into the air. They danced around the room, lingering in space before dissolving into dust when the song ended.

When the scratchy sound of the needle skipped on the record paper, it aggressively sucked me through a vortex back into this dimension. I wanted to hear the song again. I knew I had to move the needle to the start of the album, but my body wouldn't cooperate, so I stood, flapping hard. Slamming the door open, I raced over to Ethan, grabbed his arm, giving a squeeze.

He turned to Jarek and said, "Hey we're out of time."

Jarek nodded as they both put their records back and we left. I wanted to tell them I didn't need to leave; I wanted to hear the song again, but I couldn't, so when we got outside, I pushed Ethan.

Ethan kept his cool.

Jarek looked at me, asking, "What's going on?"

Ethan answered for me, stating, "He's probably hungry."

"Ahh, man, me too. Let's get some snacks." Jarek said.

We walked to the convenience store, and I went straight to my Sesame Honey Crunch. Ethan and Jarek grabbed a couple sodas, while Ethan got me a Martinelli's apple juice. Jarek wanted to get a big bag of Cheetos, but Ethan talked him into a bag of plain Lay's instead because it was the only chips Mom let me eat.

We went to pick up Alyssa since it was late already. It didn't make sense to go home, then come back out to get her. She didn't like being picked up early, but to be fair, she didn't like being picked up late, either. There was a sweet spot in the middle where she got enough time to play with friends, but didn't have to be the last one there.

Arriving home, Jarek, Ethan, and I went straight downstairs to the basement while Alyssa went to the fridge.

As usual, Ethan put on "Moving Pictures" by Rush. I liked the track "Tom Sawyer". I always wanted to read Mark Twain's work.

But for some reason, I was still hearing that New Order (Joy Division) song in my head. I wanted to tell Ethan I was sorry for grabbing and pushing him. I wanted to explain that it was a misunderstanding, that I didn't need to leave the record store. Even with Rush blasting in the background, "Ceremony" kept playing in my head, growing louder and louder.

da da da DA, da da da DA

I tuned out the other music playing and the talking. In my mind I saw words and phrases in bold letters: 'CLANDESTINE,' 'AuthentaGLOBIN,' 'DELORES,' 'PAIN,' 'HELP', 'I MISS DAD', 'I'M SORRY'.

Whenever I heard Ethan and Jarek talk about their teachers or girls, they thought were 'hot' and D&D, I wanted to join the conversation so much. I wanted to be one of the guys.

I wandered over to the ABC chart Mom posted to the wall when she was using this space as my classroom and started tapping on the letters. During my early intervention, the therapists taught me to point at things I wanted, but the skill didn't stick. I tried pointing to the letters so I could spell out the thoughts in my mind, but instead, I tapped.

As my tapping grew louder, Ethan shouted, "Hey knock it off."

I stopped for a bit, but 'Ceremony' kept playing and rising still. My head was swimming as I went over to tap again, 'clandestine', 'Delores', 'I miss Dad', 'SORRY'. I knew everything I wanted to say. It was so clear. Even though I realized they couldn't understand me, I had to do it, to tap it out for myself.

Then Jarek got off the couch, walking towards me. Though he was talking, I could only hear the song in my head. As he drew nearer, I snapped out of it, letting the real world sounds back in. Covering my ears and vocalizing, 'Ewe, you,' I tried to block out the intensity of it.

Leaning in, looking straight in my face, Jarek spoke.

"What were you doing over there?" He asked, while gesturing to the wall with the ABC chart. "I saw you spelling something."

"No, he just does that sometimes. He likes to tap on the ABC chart." Ethan said.

"No, I don't think that's what he's doing. This physical therapist who's working with my gramps came to the house a few times and she uses an ABC chart, smaller than this one. She has him point or touch letters with a pencil, so he can spell out what he wants to say." Jarek said.

It was a surreal moment; I couldn't believe that Jarek was getting what I was trying to do.

"Physical therapist?" Ethan asked.

"Yeah, physical therapist, speech therapist, massage therapist. I don't know what she is exactly. She just comes to the house and works with Gramps. It helps him. I mean, he was frustrated at first and used to throw shit, but now he does it easy." Jarek said.

"Well, that's your gramps. I don't know if Michael can do that..." Ethan said.

"Give him a chance. Don't you want him to stop grabbing and pushing and shit?" Jarek asked, interrupting.

Speechless, Ethan gestured as if to say, 'go ahead'.

Jarek turned to me and reached over to grab a pencil, then continued explaining, "This is what I saw the therapist lady do with gramps, so maybe you can give it a try."

He handed the pencil to me, and I tapped it.

"See, he doesn't know how to use it." Ethan said.

Ignoring Ethan, Jarek took my hand and steadied it. He had me hold the pencil with the tip faced backwards and the eraser towards the board.

"I'm just going to show you what to do," he said, while taking my hand and spelling out my name.

"M,I,C,H,A,E,L; got it?" Jarek asked.

"Now you try," he said, taking his hand away.

My urge was to take the pencil and turn it right side with the pointer facing out. I didn't know what to say, so I started pointing to letters 'S, T', then 'S, T', again.

"No, no. What were you trying to say before?" Jarek asked.

I started again and hit the 'S'. Jarek and Ethan looked disappointed as I messed up again, pointing to 'S', then 'T'. Knowing I was getting it wrong, something in me said to keep going and then I did it. I hit the 'O', then the 'R', then the 'R' again and then the 'Y'.

"Sorry?" Jarek asked.

I looked at him like he was Moses parting the red sea. Tapping the pencil, I started laughing while pacing in a circle.

"Come back over here." Jarek said, gesturing for me to return.

I came back and once again; he settled my hand from the tapping while gesturing for me to do it again.

"Did you mean to say 'sorry'?" He asked again.

I took the pencil and pointed to 'S,' then 'T' but then to the 'Y,' the 'E' and the 'S.'

"Oh, shit!! Did you see that?" Jarek said with enthusiasm.

"I can't believe this. Sorry for what?" Ethan asked, looking both jolted and elated.

Jarek gestured to the board so I could answer. Once again, I pointed to 'S', then 'T', then 'Q', then 'P', then 'U', then 'S', then 'H', then 'I', then 'N', then 'G'.

"I don't know what he said right there." Jarek said, turning back to Ethan.

"Pushing!" Ethan said.

Walking to the board, Ethan took the pencil out of my hand, as he demonstrated.

"See, he hits 'S, T' every time. That probably is just a, just a, like a tic or something, then he hit the 'Q' but that was a mistake because 'Q' is next to 'P', then he spells 'P,U,S,H,I,N,G', pushing. He's sorry for pushing. Remember, he pushed me outside the record store?" Ethan said, now looking towards Jarek.

"Holy SHIT, you can spell, you little MoFo," Jarek said, reaching his hand out for me to high five.

Then Alyssa came stomping downstairs.

"There's no food in the house. All I could find in the fridge was some leftover Chinese food, but it's like all plain white rice. Seriously, like 3 boxes of nothing but rice. I'm so hungry," she said, then noticing us all standing around the ABC chart. "What are you guys doing?"

"Your brother can spell!" Jarek said.

Folding her arms, un-impressed, she said, "Yeah, and?"

"No, he's talking about Michael. Michael can spell, Alyssa. He can communicate." Ethan said.

"No, duh, you guys didn't know that?" Alyssa asked with a tinge of disgust.

"Why do you think he taps on the ABC chart all the time?" She continued, gesturing to the chart.

"No, this is big Alyssa. We need to tell Mom about this!" Ethan said.

"I already tried. She didn't believe me." Alyssa said, despondently.

"No, I know, but this is different." Ethan said.

The phone rang, and Alyssa headed towards the stairs. Stopping and placing her hands on the rail, she turned back to Ethan.

"The phone's ringing. I'm not allowed to answer." She remembered.

"Oh, right." Ethan said, racing up the stairs.

"I should probably get going." Jarek said, grabbing his notebook and putting it in his backpack.

He looked at me as if he were thinking of something he wanted to say while he put his jacket and backpack on, walking to where I was standing near the ABC chart. Noticing I dropped my pencil, Jarek tried looking around for it. Unable to find it, he grabbed a crayon out of a broken mug sitting on my old desk. Giving me the crayon, he steadied my hand, so I wouldn't tap it.

Letting go, he asked me, "What was the song you listened to in the booth today?"

I started 'S', then 'T', then 'H', then 'C,E,R,E,M,O,N,Y.'

"Ceremony! Yeah, man. What band was it by?" Jarek said.

This time, I didn't hit the 'S, T' first but instead went straight to it and spelled out 'J,O,Y, D,I,V,I,S,I,O,N'

"Hah. Yeah, that's right. Wow, that's good, man." Jarek said, smirking, as Ethan came downstairs.

"That was Mom. She's working late." Ethan said.

"No, I hate when she's late." Alyssa said.

"She said she ordered us a pizza." Ethan said.

"A pizza?" Alyssa screeched.

"Yes, she said pizza." Ethan said.

"I gotta go." Jarek said, walking over to Ethan and giving him their special handshake.

Jarek started up the stairs and left as if it was any other day.

Chapter 10

SUMMER SCHOOL

In the summer of 1993, we all had summer school.

Before homeschooling, I went to something called the Extended School Year (ESY), which basically meant 'summer school.' It was an extra 4-6 weeks of school so that I wouldn't lose too much 'progress'. I didn't mind as there were little demands put on me, sometimes 4 school days instead of 5 and they were short, only about 2-3 hours. At one school we had an inflatable pool, a slip and slide, water pistols, toys, the works. We played outside all day in our bathing suits, smelling of Banana Boat sunblock that the teachers applied every hour. The only memories I have of even being in the classroom were at the end when we were greeted with the scent of cut watermelon and wrapped in warm oversized towels as we waited to be picked up by either bus or parents. I guess ,that was their idea of 'maintaining my progress' but I wasn't complaining.

Ethan and Alyssa had summer school this year for the first time, because they had missed so many days after Dad died. Jarek also had it due to moving around too much and starting school late in the year. They complained a lot.

It took a lot of pressure off Mom, as she couldn't afford summer camp. She said she owed money to the AM/PM club Alyssa attended and that the summer gave her time to 'catch up'.

I started taking the bus to and from school. I missed my walks home with Ethan and Jarek, but Mom said it wasn't fair to make Rebecca wait afterschool with me every day.

Waking earlier caused me to fall asleep faster and I've never been a good sleeper my whole life. I either rose too early, staying up too late or tossed and turned in the night due to nerves and stomach pain. At least that's what Mom thought caused it. On certain nights I remember moaning at 3am, tossing around, praying for sleep, while the pounding sensation in my head rose with each glimmer of light coming off the digital alarm clock, peering into the slits of my eyes. The pounding escalated like a Neil Peart drum solo, only not cool nor pleasant. One such night, after hearing me banging my head on the bedpost, Mom came to my aide, turning on the light, which enraged me as I lunged for her.

Dodging me, then racing into the kitchen to grab water and aspirin. She spoke softly as she handed me the medicine, "Here Michael, it's okay. Just give it a few minutes. You'll be okay."

Though the mere tickle of the fuzzy balls on my blanket felt like needles, I chose to believe her, and calmed while waiting for the aspirin to kick in. Once relief was felt, the immediate wash away of tension allowed me to lie down while Mom approached my bedside, rubbing my fingers and toes, then pressing deep into my legs and arms, as she asked if I wanted a story.

Crawling into bed with me, we snuggled close while she reached for *Black Beauty* off the nightstand, and spoke, "Let's see where were we? Did you know that Anna Sewell, the author was disabled and used horse-drawn carriage to get around much of her life? Had I mentioned that yet?"

Looking back at me, she smiled, then putting the book down on the bed massaged my head a few times before continuing the story.

So, despite the early bus mornings, I did appreciate lessening the burden on Mom. Though it was only a 20-minute walk to school, there were 8 of us, causing it to take considerably longer to deliver everyone.

A couple of my classmates didn't live at home and were dropped off at an institution. Since Ethan's school ended after mine, taking the bus bought him enough time that he could get home to meet me there.

Ethan and Jarek were always waiting outside. They'd have me go into the house, use the bathroom, then we were off.

After they discovered my ability to spell, it was like waking up from a coma and the days were awesome! We'd walk to the store, use Jarek's lunch money to buy snacks, then head to the record store, comic store or walk around talking. There was a popular highschooler hang-out on top of Kite-Hill that we frequented. Despite it being a little taxing on hot days, those were some of the best afternoons of my life.

My spelling changed everything. It wasn't even that I spelled with them all the time; it was that they knew I could and when they wanted to ask me something; they did. We'd go up to the top of the hill to sit, draw, or talk. Jarek had a small neon green alphabet and number stencil that he kept in his Pee-Chee folder. If one of them wanted to ask me something, he'd take it out, and I'd poke a pencil through the letters. It was a lot harder to use than the ABC chart at home, but I was highly motivated by the engaging conversations.

On rare occasions, they talked about Dad. Ethan was still pretty closed off about it, but Jarek had lost his dad during the Gulf War and was often the one to bring it up.

Ethan and Alyssa tried one weekend to tell Mom I knew how to spell. She was working longer hours, and it was hard to track her down, but they took her to the basement and insisted I show her. I didn't know what to spell, so I seized up, getting stuck on 'S, T'. Ethan instructed me to spell Mom's name and I tried so hard, but couldn't stop pointing to 'S, T'. I can't say why, but sometimes I get stuck in the same spot without an exit. It wasn't Mom's fault (I do this with the others too) but they already knew I could spell, so stakes weren't a s high.

I wanted so badly to tell Mom that she's terrific; that I see how much she's done for us, and I know she's lost her husband, too. I wanted to wish her 'Happy Mother's Day' for all the times I never said it. I wanted so much, but when she was there watching, I couldn't do it.

It was a little crushing as she said, "I'm glad you guys are working on this with him. That's great, but I gotta get some stuff done. Show me later if he gets it."

At night, I prayed I'd improve enough to show her the next time we got her attention.

Now that it was summertime, even with summer school, we'd need to adjust to a slightly new routine.

On the first day of ESY, I got off the bus, noticing Rebecca wasn't there to greet me as she usually was. Another classroom aide gathered us, had us grab our backpacks, and directed us to our room. Inside I could see Rebecca wasn't there either, so I stood around like a dope, not knowing what to do.

Mrs. Boulden told me to sit down in my regular seat while gesturing towards it, so I sat. I waited for 30 minutes, but no one came to sit with me, so I got up. The teacher directed me to sit back down, and I did, but after no one came, I got up again. This went on for a while and I could feel the tension building as I desperately wanted to bolt. Standing between my desk and the door, Mrs. Boulden said one more time for me to get back in my seat, but now her voice was borderline shouting and in an angry tone. I froze for a few seconds, then unfroze, opened the door, and ran out, hovering close, not knowing where to go. The blood rushed out of my head followed by intense throbbing and an avalanche of awful landing on top of me. I was in excruciating pain. At that exact moment, some students walked by; their prattling was a hammer in my head. A girl in white shorts and a pink tank top wearing a strong perfume smelled of toxic chemicals. I felt jaundice yellow toppling over with crippling nausea. The room itself started to move as Mrs. Boulden walked into the hallway and, with an angry tone, continued scolding me to return to my seat. I am ashamed to say; I lunged forward and punched the girl with strong perfume in the arm. Mrs. Boulden raced over to interfere when I grabbed her, pushing her against the wall.

I was rushed upon by a gang of teachers and students. A tall man with a mustache and a whistle around his neck wrapped my arms behind my back, forcing me to the ground, while putting his foot on my back. Pain permeated through every inch of my body as I feared one of my arms might break. I was shaking from head to toe, screaming and crying at the same time.

Next thing I knew, they were dragging me into a small room with no windows, where I was strapped to a chair.

Alone, tears streamed down my face as I cried out. The tall man poked his head in and said, "Calm down, son. I can't have you screaming like that. I'm sorry we have to restrain you. Please keep calm and keep your voice down to not disturb the other students."

Listening, I kept my voice down but was still crying, and hyperventilating with short, shallow breaths.

Briefly after, I heard a woman's voice addressing the tall man, "The mother is here already, she's in the office, we can't let her see him like this."

"What do you want me to do?" Asked the tall man.

Then I heard Mom. Her voice was unmistakable, but the words were muffled and faint. Wobbling my chair in place, I began shrieking, making as much noise as possible.

Moving closer, her voice became clear, as she questioned the man outside the door, "Is he in there?"

"Uhh," the tall man said.

"You put him in a friggin' closet? What's wrong with you people?" Mom asked rhetorically, hurtling open the door.

Catching one sight of me, Mom burst into tears, racing over, immediately unbuckling the restraints.

"Oh, baby. Are you okay?" She asked, holding me tight.

In Mom's arms, I released a long stream of tears unlike any I had before. The sobs came from deep within my soul, summoning all the sadness of all the years of pathological loneliness. I felt all the shame of being a person who did things that hurt others. I felt all the embarrassment from the times people stared, pointed, name called and otherwise rejected me or chalked me up to being no better than an animal.

I was terrified. Mom was more than understanding about things like this, but Dad got angry. He called me a 'bully' and told me that I was going to be drugged or taken away if I acted like this. I was terrified of that happening, but more than that, I wanted to please him. Even though he was gone, I knew he could still see me, and he must be so disappointed, if not furious, with me.

Mom took me home, staying with me the rest of the day. Feeling lethargic, I laid in bed. Hearing Ethan, Jarek and Alyssa arriving, a huge lump appeared in my throat, realizing they would soon know what I did.

Then I heard Mom tell Ethan, "Michael can't go back to the ESY. I'm probably going to have to change the schedule around a bit."

"Why? What happened?" Ethan asked.

"Just a staffing situation. I will tell you more tomorrow, after I talk to my boss. Okay?" Mom said.

It was quiet for a minute before I heard Jarek walk out of the bathroom when Mom descended on him in the hallway.

"Hey Jarek. What were you saying about the physical therapist that works with your grandpa?" Mom asked.

"Uhm, I don't really remember." Jarek said.

"You know when you said she gives him massage and helps him communicate? You even said she recommends diet, vitamins, herbs. Stuff like that?" Mom said.

"Oh yeah, right. Grandma thinks she's crazy though. I don't know if any of that stuff works." Jarek said.

"No, I know you don't, but I'm just wondering if you can tell me how to get in touch with her." Mom said.

"Grandma? You can just come by anytime you want; she never goes anywhere..." Jarek said.

"No, your grandpa's physical therapist." Mom said, interrupting.

"Oh, right. Uhm. To tell you the truth, I don't even know. I can't remember her name; I was only there a couple times when she came by, and I don't think she comes by at all anymore. Gramps is military, so he gets whatever they want to pay for. If they decide to stop paying for physical therapy, he don't get no more..." Jarek said.

"Okay, I get it." Mom said.

Mom made a sound like she was about to say something, then paused, before asking, "Do you really think that Michael can spell? You know, like your grandpa, or gramps?"

"With all due respect, Mrs. Hogan, I know he can." Jarek said.

Chapter 11

THE C.R.O. REPORT

After the incident at school, Mom told her boss I was sick and she needed to stay home for the rest of the week.

We picked up Alyssa from school, which meant Ethan and Jarek didn't need to rush home and watch us. As a result, they took off straight after their summer classes and were rarely seen around the house. I imagined they were off doing cool things like we did last Spring.

I hoped we'd have these few days to do something fun, but Mom was afraid to take me anywhere after what happened, and we stayed home most of the time.

Alyssa always had friends over, either from school or around the neighborhood. Mom set up an inflatable pool in the backyard and kept the sprinklers on so we could play in them. Alyssa and her friends ran in and out of the house, leaving a trail of water and melted popsicles everywhere they went.

Mom stayed busy watching them and taking care of things around the house that had been neglected since she started working. Over the weekend, she tracked down Ethan and told him they had to set up a 'plan of attack' for her returning to work.

"Why can't he go back to summer school?" Ethan barked with irritation.

"I told you already. That's not an option." Mom said.

"Well, I have 3 more weeks of classes, so what do you want me to do?" Ethan asked, growing more irritated.

"I don't know. I'll take him with me on Monday and see if there's a way for me to get the mornings off, at least until your summer classes end." Mom said, considering the options. "I still need you to watch them after that."

"Yes, I am aware." Ethan said.

"I'm sorry you feel put upon. I'm just trying to get us through this." Mom said.

"I know." he said, leaving the dining room, and heading down to the basement.

On Monday, Mom took me to work with her. This was the second time I had been there, including that day she got the job. Upon arrival, she straightened my shirt, brushed some lint off, and fixed my hair. Then said, "I know you can be a gentleman while we're here and behave yourself, okay?"

I looked at her, blinking my eyes to tell her I was listening. Taking a deep breath, she checked herself in the review mirror and headed out of the car.

I followed her to the front of the building, which was just as dark and grey as I remembered. There wasn't anyone outside like last time. Mom typed a code into the metal number pad by the door, causing it to make a click as she opened quickly and held it for me to walk inside.

Making our way to Mom's desk, which was in front of Dr. Cody's office. There was a partition wrapped around it, giving some privacy. She looked so professional: having her own desk, computer, and phone. Waiting for her lead, she instructed me to sit in a chair next to hers. Looking back at Dr. Cody's office, then back at hers, she started shuffling papers around, until the phone rang, answering, "Dr. Cody McDougal's office."

I couldn't hear what the other person was saying, just some muffled words and something about an appointment. Mom hung up, wrote on a message pad, ripped it off, then walked to Dr. Cody's office and knocked.

"Come in," his voice said.

Mom opened the door, and I followed as we walked inside. Dr. Cody had his head down, staring at a document on his lap while talking on the phone. His glasses were on top of his head, like a headband, the way Mom wore her sunglasses all the time.

Speaking into the phone, Dr. Cody said, "The results were unexpected. Less than optimal is fair to say... that was the CRO report."

Mom placed the message on Dr. Cody's desk and escorted me out of his office. There was that acronym again '**CRO**.' They use acronyms in school all the time. It's like their own little code language. They might say things like IEP, IFSP, IEE, SLP, SDC and so on. I knew I was supposed to be quiet, but my body took over as I started laughing. Dr. Cody immediately looked at me and then over at Mom. He appeared stunned, if not unhappy, about my being there.

"I'm sorry, can I call you back?" Dr. Cody said.

We proceeded out of the office and Mom shut the door, directing me to sit in the chair next to hers again.

A few moments later, Dr. Cody opened the door and said to Mom, "Bridgett, I'm off the phone. Can you come in here a minute?"

Mom got up and instructed me to stay in the chair, though I got up anyway. She guided me to sit down again by patting the chair and saying, "Come on, Michael, right here. Stay here."

I sat at first, but once Mom walked into Dr. Cody's office, I couldn't sit there alone and got up to follow her.

As I was walking towards the door, I could hear Dr. Cody ask, "What's going on?"

"There was a problem at the school and unfortunately I don't have a back-up." Mom said.

"Problem? What sort of problem?" Dr. Cody asked.

"You know, budget cuts, there was a staffing issue, and they don't have an aide for him," Mom said.

"Ah, so do you think it's appropriate to bring him here?" Dr. Cody asked.

"No, of course not. I just wanted to come in and ask if I could take off the mornings for the next few weeks while my older son, Ethan, is in summer school. Once he's finished, he can watch Michael." Mom said.

The whole time they were speaking, Dr. Cody kept his eyes on me. He reminded me of what I thought a nutty professor might look like. His remaining hair was disheveled, and the suit wrinkled like last time. In fact, it was the same suit. Even though he was a big-time science guy, he had this look on his face, like he was perpetually confused. He didn't sit still in his chair but always pushed it back, then crouched forward as he spoke. He was funny to me. I started laughing again.

"You got a joke for us?" He said as my laughing grew. "I'll be on vacation starting next week. You are the best assistant I have ever had, but, uhm, I guess so Bridgett if you need to. But just so you know, I'm not interested in a part-time assistant."

"Yes, of course not. This is just for a couple weeks." Mom said, elated.

Still scrutinizing me, Dr. Cody continues, "You know my brother, I told you about my brother. He's uhm, I told you about him, right? I mean, yeah, take the mornings, but just for the next few weeks. I'll be on vacation next week, for two weeks."

"Yes, Doctor I remember." Mom said.

"So, you know, it's uhm, I take my family to, every year we do a thing, so," Dr. Cody said.

"Sounds lovely." Mom said with great relief.

The rest of the week after Mom and I took Alyssa to school, we went to the store before heading home. We had food stamps now and the closest store that accepted them was a large chain out of town. Mom made sure (as much as possible), that our fridge was stocked as now that she was taking mornings off, she was returning home later than ever.

I liked it being the two of us in the morning. It felt almost like it was before, but without Dad, there was a perpetual void.

The following Monday after dropping off Alyssa, Mom turned to me and said she needed to go to work, which confused me since she told Dr. Cody that she'd be taking mornings off while Ethan was still in summer school.

When we arrived, I noticed the office was less crowded than normal. There was no one at the front desk, allowing us to walk straight past and into Mom's space. Sitting in her swivel chair, she took a key from the top drawer, then used it to open Dr. Cody's office. After she headed inside, I followed, then she locked the door behind us.

Since Dr. Cody was on vacation, it was empty but looked the same; messy with papers piled high in trays and documents sitting on top of his computer keyboard. The office smelled of leather and freshly printed paper and was cold, despite the hot summer day.

Mom sat in Dr. Cody's chair, took the documents off his computer, and started typing.

"I know you are in here." She said, talking to the computer.

She was typing fast and had a deep, studying furrow in her brow. I wandered over to where she was and stood behind her, trying to read what she was typing.

"NDAs, my ass." Mom said with eyes fixated on the computer page.

I still couldn't make out what she was typing, but had a feeling it had something to do with Dad.

This went on for a while as I grew restless, wandering around the room, stealing a pen for tapping that rested on a stack of papers near the edge of Dr. Cody's desk. As I took it, the stack and a bunch of other stuff fell to the floor. Mom turned, looking to see what happened, then kneeled while picking up the fallen items.

"This is a bit of a mess." She said, picking up the papers that were now all out of order. "Good thing Cody is a slob; he won't know the difference."

Stopping to take notice, she began reading.

"What is this? A CRO report on... On what? It's so cryptic." Mom said, eyes still fixated on the page.

With my interest peaked hearing that for the third time, I peered over Mom's shoulder while she kneeled on the floor reading.

There it was, the CRO report; phrases and words jumped off the page,

'Blood transfusion', 'myocardial infarction' and others I couldn't make sense of.

Mom stood, dropping the pages to the floor, placing her hand over her mouth while making a muffled scream.

Pointing to the document on the floor, she said out loud. "I can't believe it,"

Walking over to see where she was pointing, I saw Dad's name; there it was among others it said Dr. John Hogan. What did Dad have to do with this report?

Picking up the papers, Mom looked at me, "Come on, Let's go,"

Walking over to her desk, she placed the document in a copy machine sitting on the other side of the room. Then a head popped up around the partition.

"Hey Bridgett, I didn't know you were here." Said the woman who was at the front desk the first day we came.

"I'm not. I just needed to come in and copy a few things." Mom said.

The woman came around, leaning up against Mom's desk, half sitting on it, while holding a coffee cup wafting the smell of caramel candy.

"This place is dead. Skeleton staff for summer. I'm taking next week too. You?" The woman asked.

"No, I haven't been here long enough for vacation time; I'm just taking mornings to watch Michael." Mom said, gesturing towards me.

"Oh, well, I'll let you get back to it." The woman said, glancing at me with recognition.

As she walked away, Mom looked back with a sigh of relief, gathering the copied documents and putting the originals back in Dr. Cody's office before locking his door.

Gesturing for me to come with her, we left and got back in the car.

Inside, Mom sat quietly for a minute, wiped a bead of sweat from her forehead, then rested it on the steering wheel.

"Between you and me, Michael, I don't know about this place. Dad worked here for almost a year, and I've been here for several months, but I still don't even know what they do. Whatever it is, it seems shady. What was his name doing on that report?" She said, slamming her hands on the steering wheel.

Banging the steering wheel a few more times, she took a deep breath, then drove as we went to pick up Alyssa.

Chapter 12

THE CONFRONTATION

Later that day, I still hadn't shaken off what I saw at Dr. Cody's office and Mom's reaction to it. I couldn't believe all this time Mom had been searching for answers about Dad. I mean, it made sense, but she managed to keep it to herself quite well.

Ethan and Jarek arrived a few moments later. I began flapping and laughing.

"Hi boys, I need to go. I'm already late," Mom said.

"You need to go?" Alyssa asked, distressed.

"You know I do, honey," Mom said, as Alyssa ran up and gave her a hug.

"Ethan, if you could, keep an eye on Alyssa and her friends. Just poke your head out of the basement occasionally to make sure they haven't started a fire or anything." Mom said while she was cutting vegetables and putting them in the slow cooker. "Did you hear me?"

"Yes, watch Alyssa and her friends," Ethan said.

"Okay, bye, honey." Mom said as she closed the slow cooker, grabbed her briefcase off the dining room table, then proceeded down the hall.

She took her purse off the coat rack while fishing through it, pulling out her sunglasses and keys.

"You guys got everything? Be good, okay." Mom said.

"We will, Mom." Alyssa said.

Ethan shrugged.

"Have a good day, Mrs. Hogan," Jarek said as Mom waved, kissing Alyssa on the forehead, then left.

Ethan signaled to Jarek, and they started for the basement as I followed.

"Aren't you going to give me my lunch before going downstairs?" Alyssa asked.

"You had your lunch already," Ethan said, continuing downstairs.

When we got to the basement, he turned on the radio while Jarek plopped down, throwing his weighty backpack on the floor. He started saying something, then stopped, noticing me by the ABC chart.

"Oh, hey, man. You got something to say?" He asked, walking over, grabbing a pencil, and handing it to me, then gesturing to the chart as if to say, 'Go ahead.'

Starting out 'S, T,' then 'C, R, O,'. Jarek said the letters out loud as I pointed.

"CRO?" Jarek asked, puzzled.

Again, I spelled 'C,R,O,' then 'R,E,P,O,R,T.'

"What's that?" Jarek asked.

I didn't know how to answer that question, so I went back to poking, 'S, T', then 'B, C, Q, R, T, O'.

Truthfully, I still didn't know what the CRO report was, but if Dad's name was on it, I wanted to know more. Was it his last project?

What is a myocardial infarction? Dr. Cody said they worked on projects; was this one of those? Is he hiding something?

"Uhm, man, I don't really know what you're trying to say right now. Let's try again later, alright?" Jarek said, patting me on the shoulder, heading to the couch, pulling out a comic from his backpack.

"Man, I got this yesterday…" Jarek started as I tapped loudly on the ABC chart.

Jarek and Ethan both came over to where I was standing, looking puzzled. Ethan grabbed the pencil this time and put it in my hand.

"What's going on?" He asked with concern.

I knew this was important, so I took a long pause when Ethan finally said, gesturing to the board, "Get it . . ."

I began pointing, 'S, T,' then I spelled, 'D,A,D'. "Dad? What about Dad?" Ethan asked.

I kept spelling, 'D,A,D,S, R,E,P,O,R,T . . . ' Then Jarek took a crayon and a piece of paper off the desk and started writing as I spelled. He said the letters out loud one by one, then wrote the word.

Ethan took the pencil from my hand, then gave it back to me, telling me to continue.

I spelled 'M,O,M', as Jarek said out loud, "M,O,M, Mom."

Then I spelled 'H,A,S, D,A,D,S, L,A,S,T, R,E,P,O,R,T'.

Ethan took the pencil from my hand as Jarek said out loud, "Mom, has Dad's last report?"

Ethan, looking puzzled, asked, "So, what's the big deal about Dad's last report?"

I continued spelling and tried to spell out myocardial infarction, but they couldn't understand and figured I was making a bunch of mistakes.

"Sounds like your mom is doing some investigative work. Didn't you say that she didn't believe your dad died of a heart-attack? I mean,

I've asked around and ain't no one in this town know what that big building does." Jarek said.

Ethan looked perplexed while Jarek threw his hands up and said, "I'm just saying!"

Handing the pencil back to me, Ethan asked, "What is on the report?"

He quickly drew the pencil back and thought for a second, then handed it back to me, asking, "Where did Mom get the report?"

I spelled 'D,R, C,O,D,Y' as Jarek said each letter out loud while I wrote it down in a notebook.

After I was finished, I dropped the pencil on the floor. Jarek handed the notebook to Ethan.

Ethan looked down at the page, thought for a moment, then read it out loud, "Dr. Cody?"

"Who's Dr. Cody?" Jarek asked.

"It's my mom's boss." Ethan said.

"See, that's what I'm sayin.' Your mom is a double agent. Damn. She's stealing files from her boss. That's gangsta." Jarek said.

"If this is true, she could be putting her job, herself... hell, us in jeopardy," Ethan said.

"Only if they have something to hide." Jarek said.

"Still, it's risky. She could at the very least lose her job, even go to jail, and then where will we be?" Ethan asked, throwing his hands in the air.

"From what you told me, this place kicked your dad to the curb, then refused to offer any help or even information about why." Jarek said.

"I need to confront her about this." Ethan said.

"Oh, I'm not missing this. I'm calling Grams to tell her I'm spending the night!" Jarek said, racing upstairs.

The rest of the day was excruciatingly long. Ethan and Jarek tried to play D&D, but they were exceedingly distracted and started making all kinds of wild accusations.

"Hey, what if your dad discovered something shady going on in that building and they wacked him?" Jarek abruptly asked.

"Come on, man. Let's not take it there. We are just trying to figure out why he got fired and why he didn't tell us." Ethan said.

"Exactly!" Jarek said.

At around 8:30pm, Alyssa fell asleep on the couch, so Ethan carried her to bed. We were used to Mom working late, but this was especially late, and I was feeling anxious. I wasn't trying to speculate about anything at this point, but nevertheless, Mom's tardiness was worrying.

Ethan, Jarek and I sat on the couch watching Friday the 13TH. I'm not much for horror movies, but this was a particularly terrible choice under the circumstances. Around 9pm, we heard Mom pull up in the driveway; when she came into the house as usual, she dropped her keys, briefcase, sunglasses, and coffee mug on the dining room table.

I jumped off the couch, and Ethan followed, walking over to the dining room while Jarek stayed on the couch, turning around to see the action. Noticing all eyes on her, Mom stopped, surveying the situation.

"What's going on? Is everything okay?" She asked.

Before we could respond, she noticed Jarek on the couch asking, "Do you live here now?"

"Grams said I could sleep over." Jarek said with a smile.

"Are you guys having a pow-wow? What's up?" She said.

"Why are you stealing Dad's reports from Dr. Cody's office?" Ethan asked.

"What are you talking about?" Mom asked.

"You know what I'm talking about, Mom. This could be dangerous, stealing confidential files." Ethan said.

Mom, looking utterly stunned and confused, took a step back, then glanced at all of us trying to figure out how we knew. Gasping with both hands to her mouth, she looked at me as if she had seen a ghost.

She asked, though her eyes said she already knew the answer, "How do you... It's not what you guys are thinking, it's just some work I'm doing from home."

"What's a CRO report?" Ethan said.

Her brow furrowed, her lips pursed as she brought both hands to her mouth, again shaking her head 'no'. She sat at the dining room table, retrieving the CRO report from her briefcase.

"I had this locked in my briefcase. How did you see it?" Mom asked.

"Mom, I didn't see it. Michael did." Ethan said.

Mom started nodding her head, 'yes', then began to cry. Turning to me, she whispered, "Sorry," then hugged me tight.

"I'm sorry. I didn't believe it. It's true; it's really true. You've been here all along." She said, pulling away, taking my face in her hands.

Hugging me still, I hugged back. In a split second, an ocean of thoughts raced through my mind, cataloging the events of my life from my earliest memories, when I was 2 and the doctor told Mom I was going to live in an institution, to the bullies at the ice-skating rink shouting 'you're weird' in unison, to the tears streaming down my face as I sat strapped to a chair in the closet at school and on it went to the present moment. I breathed a sigh of relief that Mom finally knew I was smart. Taking a deep breath, she smiled, wiping the tears from her face.

Sliding the CRO report across the table so we could all see, she began, "A CRO is a Contact Research Organization. It's no secret document. It's an outside organization that provides clinical trial management for drug makers."

"I don't know what you just said." Jarek said, chiming in.

"Is he okay to be here for this conversation?" Mom asked Ethan while pointing at Jarek.

"Ah, no need to worry, Mrs. Hogan. I'm great at keeping secrets." Jarek said.

"Well . . . that's fine, but I don't know that there's a secret here." She said, combing through the pages of the document.

"A CRO is just a third party that evaluates clinical research data and helps the drug manufacturers chances of getting the product approved by regulators, so that it can be put on the market." Mom said.

"So why was Dad named in the report?" Ethan asked.

"Well, that's what I wanted to know. See, I've been looking for information on why your father was let go, but it's all locked under the non-disclosure agreement. I can't find his name on anything. It's like he never worked there at all. I dug through documents, computer files, anything I can get my hands on, but this was the first time I saw his name. It didn't make sense to me, and I could hardly understand most of what's in there. They speak in codes, half the document is acronyms, it's worse than an IEP meeting. I've been going to the library looking through science and medical texts just to understand what these words even mean." Mom said.

When Mom first started mentioning that she didn't believe Dad's cause of death was a heart attack, everyone dismissed her and chalked it up to grief. After a while she gave up talking about it but not on seeking answers, which I thought was brave.

"What's this about blood transfusions?" Ethan asked, picking up the stack of papers from the table.

"The report is evaluating a trial by a company called 'Authenta-GLOBIN,' they're creating an artificial blood to be used during transfusions," she said.

"It says clandestine. That's a military term, isn't it?" Jarek said.

"It means, done in secret. This report is evaluating a trial that was done on patients without their knowledge or consent, trading out normal donor blood for this artificial blood," she said.

"Ahh . . . man, that sounds like a bad idea." Jarek said.

"It was a bad idea." She said, skimming through the document to find a certain page. "See it says here."

"It just says: highly significant differences." Ethan said, reading the highlighted area she was pointing at.

"I know, and those significant differences were a 42 percent increase of adverse reactions. In this section, it says that 10 out of 81 recipients of the artificial blood died of a heart attack, while none of 71 recipients who received normal donor blood died." Mom said.

"What? Could Dad have received this blood, causing his heart attack? I mean, he did have surgery. Don't you need a transfusion during surgery?" Ethan asked, becoming increasingly distressed.

"Sometimes, but I have no way of knowing. The hospital won't give me any of Dad's records due to privacy laws," she said.

"Holy shit, this is bullshit," Ethan said, building hostility.

"Excuse you... Language." Mom said.

"But still, why is Dad's name in the document?" Ethan asked.

"All it says is that the data analysis from Dr. John Hogan was 'not needed' and therefore removed from the report. That's it. I don't know where to find his data analysis or why it was removed or if that's even significant. I don't want you guys getting all excited. I thought maybe I had found something, but to tell you the truth, I really don't know. I think maybe I just wanted to find something, anything to do with your dad, that I just thought this might be important." She said.

"Pardon me for chiming in but what if Mr. Hogan found something bad, and they didn't like what he had to say about it?" Jarek said, then turning to Ethan continued, "You always say he was such a straight arrow. Maybe it wasn't a heart attack or a weird blood transfusion."

"That's an interesting theory, Jarek, but this report already looks bad. How could it have been any worse?" Mom asked, as if she had already thought of everything.

"I don't know, but why was it done in secret?" Jarek asked.

"Because, given a choice, who's going to participate in this willingly?" Mom said.

"Well, you can't give up! You have to keep looking! We have to keep looking! What about Dad? This is such bullshit," Ethan said, growing angry as his eyes welled with tears.

The pain emanating from him, as if finally coming to the fore, was palpable. Mom got up to hug Ethan, but he swatted her hands away. Not one to give up, she went in again, as he received her, allowing the tears to roll down his face.

At the time, it felt like a cathartic moment, but little did we know then that this was the tip of the iceberg.

Chapter 13

THE NEW LIBERATOR

After Ethan confronted Mom, the atmosphere at home was much lighter. Mom stopped working so late and came home straight away to have dinner with us. After dinner, we went downstairs to practice my spelling in the basement. She came up with this idea to read articles from the newspaper and highlight certain words, she called my 'spelling words'. I'd start off with the spelling words, then she'd ask me a question or two about what the article was about. Sometimes Alyssa joined spelling too.

After summer school ended, Ethan slept until noon or so and Mom started working mornings again, while Alyssa kept an eye on things. If one of us got hungry or needed a band-aid, she'd wake him up. Jarek still came over every day, and we'd all hang out.

One Saturday, Mom took us to the movies. Ethan and Jarek saw *The Last Action Hero,* while Mom, Alyssa and I saw *Dennis the Menace.*

It was a long time since we had been to a movie or done anything together as a family, for that matter. When I was a little kid, we went often, but because I wasn't used to the loud sound, I had such a hard time sitting through an entire showing. Mom or Dad needed to take me outside and walk me around to avoid a scene. This led Mom to believe that I didn't like movies and when one of my therapists asked her to name something I didn't like, she told her. 'The movies'. The therapist was trying to teach me to answer 'yes or no' questions, so she thought if she knew something I didn't like and asked me about it, I should definitely say 'no'. The only problem was that I DID like the movies, so when the therapist asked, 'Do you like the movies?' I said 'Yes.' The therapist quickly directed my hand to answer 'no', saying in a slow monotone voice, 'NO, you don't like the movies'. I continued to answer 'yes', every time she asked, as her corrections went on a long while, funny it never occurred to anyone that I did in fact enjoy the ci nema.

Thank goodness Mom finally figured it out. While it was a rough road, it felt like I had a chance for a bright future ahead.

One afternoon, Ethan, Alyssa, and I met Jarek at the record store. Walking there, the heat was oppressive; Alyssa complained, "How much longer? I can't take this anymore."

The moistness filled me from the nap of my neck down to the bottoms of my flat feet, causing the rubber from my flip-flops to cling to them.

"Stop being annoying, we're like, right there," Ethan said, pointing to glass doors that stood 20 feet away.

Racing up ahead, Alyssa whooshed open the doors, releasing the air-conditioned cool, alongside the pounding sound of Jane's Addiction's "Stop", which erupted in a boom with a pulsating rhythm, then came down raining fireworks.

Taking my hand, Alyssa dragged me to the pop music section as she furiously combed through the records like she was on a mission, finally settling on an album with four beautiful women on the cover.

Whisking me away over to where Ethan was browsing through the rock and grunge section, she said, "We want to listen to this one!"

"Good for you," he said, without looking up. With the record in one hand and the other on her hip, Alyssa tapped her foot on the floor, staring Ethan down until he looked over at her while pointing towards the sound booth. "Listen over there."

Smiling at her victory, Alyssa gestured for me to follow her as we headed for the sound booth. Gingerly removing the record from its sleeve and placing it on the turntable, Alyssa turned to me with a gleam of excitement on her face. To my surprise, the track started with strong A Capella vocal, then broke into a catchy love-gone-wrong song.

Once the beat took hold, the floor vibrated as I swayed from side to side. Snatching my hands up, Alyssa swayed with me and as we started getting into our groove, Ethan's banging on the booth window gave us a start, causing our dance to cease.

Opening the booth door, Ethan stated, "Let's go," then walked away without explanation. "I don't want to go!" Alyssa yells, still inside the booth.

Ethan turns around reminding her, "Hey, it's your friend coming over that we have to get back for."

"Oh right," she said, clamoring to put the record back in the sleeve, then handed it to Ethan.

Jarek stood in the doorway, leaning up against it, waiting for the rest of us while taking the record from his hand and putting it in his backpack.

When we arrived home, Alyssa's friend Laura was waiting, wearing a backpack and holding her mother's hand. Alyssa ran to Laura, squeezing her while lifting her up off the ground.

"This, okay?" Laura's mom asked Ethan, gesturing to Laura as she ran into the house with Alyssa.

"Yes, it's okay. I watch them all the time. I'm CPR certified. Mom will be home in a couple hours," he said, comforting the mom.

Smiling and nodding her head, Laura's mom pokes inside the house, waving to her daughter. "Bye, sweetie."

"Bye, Mom," Laura answers as she and Alyssa run into her room, shutting the door behind them.

Finally, alone in the basement, Jarek excitedly plops down on the couch, pulling the newly purchased album out of his backpack. The cover art had two little girls, smiling with fairy wings. The title read "Smashing Pumpkins - Siamese Dreams". I wasn't sure if the two girls were actual Siamese twins or trying to look like it, but the strange title only added intrigue.

"Dale said this band was heavily influenced by Rush," Jarek said eagerly as he took it out and placed it on the turntable.

"Hell yeah." Ethan said.

Flicking my fingers in front of my face, I paced with anticipation. The first track drew me in with a drum roll, then an urgent guitar rift. Once his distinct vocals started in with a pleading cry, 'let me out, LET ME OUT,' we all knew this was going to be epic. Each track spoke to me in such a way that I believed they were written for me; with this overarching theme that crooned of waking up and breaking free.

"This is da' bomb, but I can't say I hear the Rush influence." Ethan said.

"I can kind of hear it. Those drums, man." Jarek said.

"Yeah, but Neil Peart?" Ethan said.

"I know, I know. Still, it's dope." Jarek said.

By the time we got to track four, I was already sure this was my new favorite album. "Hummer" caught my attention, sounding like a cross between an exotic instrument and a scratched record. When the vocals began, I hung on each word.

I could no longer hear Ethan and Jarek's chattering. Or maybe they were silent. I heard the music only, as the room went black with a fog surrounding me, standing near the speaker. The rip-roaring rock went soft and reflective, while the vocals cooed the final time.

Once the instrumental stanza began, the surrounding clouds became a swirl of colors wrapping around and dripping from my flicking fingers like melted butter. No, not butter, perhaps wax or melted frosting, or something in between. Immersed in its beauty, the watercolor sound escaped my fingers and waved across my body with tiny musical notes that whooshed and hung like debris in the wind.

By the end, we were all quiet. Standing near the speaker, I could see Ethan and Jarek sitting on the couch in awe. I was in such a state I barely heard Alyssa bounding down the stairs.

She looked around and abruptly asked, "What got into you guys? You look like you've been punched in the face?"

After a few moments of silence, bouncing off the couch, Jarek said, "That was epic!"

Ethan and Jarek started high-fiving, shaking hands, and laughing like there were kids who just walked out of Disneyland.

"Okay, whatever freaks. Mom just called," Alyssa said.

"You're not supposed to answer the phone," Ethan said.

"I know, I didn't. It went to the machine. She said she's going to be late and is ordering us a pizza." Alyssa said, before walking back up the stairs.

"Did she say if she paid with credit card?" Ethan asked.

"No." Alyssa said.

"I better go see if she left me some money." Ethan said as we followed Alyssa.

Making his way to the dining room, and the dresser where Mom kept the kitchen appliances, including the waffle maker; Ethan rummaged through the top drawer, pulling out a box of paperclips, a roll of stamps, post-it notes, random staples, and then finally the newsletter David from Country Life Harvest gave Mom all those months ago.

Then the doorbell rang, followed by excessive knocking.

"Hey bro, what's up?" Jarek said, opening the door.

"Mellow on the knocking. Hey, I hope my mom already paid, cuz I don't have any cash." Ethan said, pulling alongside Jarek standing in the doorway.

"Yeah, figures," the pizza guy said, pulling the pie out of the insulator and handing it to Ethan.

"Oh, so I guess she did," Ethan said, taking it to the dining room table.

"She didn't leave a tip, though," the pizza guy said, holding his hand out in front of Jarek.

"Ah, dude, let me see," Jarek said, stuffing his hands in his pockets, then pulling $5 out, says, "All I got is a five."

"I'll take it," the pizza guy said, snatching the 5 out of Jarek's hand and heading back down the walkway.

"That's too much, bro," Jarek calls out before shaking his head, then shutting the door.

"Alyssa and Alyssa's friend... Pizza's here!" Ethan shouted, then we all gathered around the dining room table, as everyone but me dived into the meal, leaving no crumb left in the box.

"Gah, there's nothing left for Michael?" Ethan said as he took a slice off his plate, handing it to me.

"It's those little girls. They took like half the pie," Jarek said, gesturing to Alyssa's room.

Barreling into Alyssa's room, Ethan went to retrieve the excess food as Jarek and I sat at the table.

"What's this?" Jarek said, studying the newsletter Ethan left on the table.

"I don't know, just some junk." Ethan said, attempting to pull it out of Jarek's hand.

"Nah man, let me read it. There's something in here." Jarek said, studying more intently.

"Like what? Victoria Secrets ads?" Ethan said, leaning in to see the paper. "Ahh, it's just a newsletter."

Still intently reading, Jarek places his hand on his chin, stroking his few strands of chin hair, then with eyes wide looks over at us, shaking his head.

"Dude, isn't that what your mom was talking about the other night? You know the fake blood story?"

Jarek said, pointing to the article in the paper while sliding it over for us to see, then reading for a few seconds, Ethan says, "Yeah, it is. That is weird."

"That's it? You don't see the writing on the wall here, man?" Jarek said.

"What writing? It's weird but I'm sure the story must have got out." Ethan said.

"Dude, no, you don't get it. Look at the date. It's months before your mom told us about it," Jarek said, as Ethan snatched the paper back, looking closer. "It's before your dad…"

"Died." Ethan said. "It doesn't make any sense."

"The only explanation is that someone on the inside is feeding information to these people." Jarek said pulling the newsletter back, then turning the pages, revealing the headline: 'Girl sold by drug-addicted parents to science.' "It also means, that if this is true, what else in here might be?"

A chill moved up my spine as my thoughts went to Mom, wondering why she was late and when she'd be home.

Chapter 14

ATOP KITE-HILL

After summer, I ended up going back to school. Mom informed me she had been in touch with them and was able to resolve the issue. I don't know what she said, but now I not only had Rebecca as my aide, but also a myriad of therapists working with me.

The speech therapist sat with me during lunch, teaching me the signs of all the items in my lunchbox. If I wanted the apple slices, she'd have me sign 'apple' and if I wanted 'more', I needed to sign 'more'. Sign language was fascinating and pretty to watch. I enjoyed learning it, though it was difficult. My head saw it clearly, but my hands refused to place in the proper positions. Nevertheless, this lunch experience was degrading, feeling a bit like a dog begging for a biscuit. If she had come during any other activity, it might have been better, or maybe that's asking too much. I don't know.

In addition to Speech, there was Occupation therapy (OT) and Adaptive Physical Education (APE). The APE was fun as my teacher, Jean took me to play basketball whereas OT was hit or miss. Some activities were tough, like when I was forced to write.

"No, you must not help him. If he wants to write, he will." Usha the OT said to Rebecca as she attempted to give my hand pressure while spelling my name.

"No, I know, but I'm just giving a little pressure. I'm not doing it for him. I feel him doing it when I just push against his arm. Like this." Rebecca said, demonstrating how she leaned her hand against my forearm when I wrote.

Usha stood with arms crossed, her mouth in a neutral position with one eyebrow lifted as if to ask who Rebecca thought she was, taking liberties, being only an aide.

"Uh, I know that's not. It's just, I saw some of the other aides doing it and I figured it works for him." Rebecca said in response to the eyebrow, noting that the students with cerebral palsy and visual impairments were assisted, though if she helped me, it was thought of as 'cheating'.

Without another word, Usha took the pencil from my hand and sat in Rebecca's seat, forcing her to leap out of it.

I did like the OT's squeeze machine or when she had me pull objects out of Playdough, those were somewhat relaxing.

Mom continued to practice spelling with me using articles from the newspaper, but she only did it on the weekends, as she started working late again. Sometimes during these sessions, I'd go rogue and try to ask her about Dad or what she was doing at work. If I made a mistake and poked the wrong letter one time, it would throw the whole thing off and Mom would have me start over. With Ethan and Jarek, though, I was communicating freely. Mom printed up several alphabet charts on regular 8x10 paper and laminated them at work. Ethan and Jarek both kept one in their backpacks so they could ask me questions anytime. If I was having a meltdown, they could come over and ask what was wrong. It's beyond difficult to express what you're feeling when you're in distress, but it's a skill I'm working on.

Ethan, Jarek and I read the New Liberator religiously.

"This right here. I can't get over this story." Jarek said, pointing to a headline '34 microbiologist and geneticist suicided or missing' in the newsletter as we trekked up the dry dirt path on Kite-Hill.

Based on the articles we read, we came up with multiple conspiracy theories about Dad. The top three were 1) he was given the artificial blood in the hospital, and it caused his heart attack, 2) he was murdered for telling the truth about it and 3) there was an elaborate scheme to fake his death so he could be taken and used to experiment on bio-weapons. Admittedly, we had no evidence to support these claims, especially the last one, but I wanted that one to be true because if Dad was still alive, we could see him again.

"It doesn't make sense." Ethan said.

"Of course it does; your dad could be one of these scientists." Jarek said.

I went back to riding the bus home from school while Ethan and Jarek were always waiting. We took that hike up Kite-Hill most afternoons to hang with friends. Jason carried a yellow glow, which normally made me a little uncomfortable, but I liked him and needed to keep an open mind about people who didn't have the most appealing glow.

"Nirvana are already legends. They are waaaayyy better than The Pumpkins. Give me a break." Jason said.

"What? Are you for real?" Ethan said.

"What do you think?" Jason asked, turning to me, as Ethan lifted my alphabet board and gestured for me to spell.

'S,T.' I started as Ethan karate chopped my board and made me start again.

'N,O,T, S,U,R,E', I spelled in an attempt to stay neutral. I can't say I care for politics.

"Ah, have some balls, man." Jason said, jibbing me.

"Grunnggge is dea, dea, dea, dead!" Our other friend Darnel said, then rapped something about fat asses.

When Darnel rapped, his stutter went away, while his greenish glow popped on and off to his perfect beat.

Since I started spelling, Ethan wasn't as embarrassed by me and even appeared somewhat proud. He liked showing his friends how I could spell on the alphabet board, and they loved asking me questions. Mostly they talked about girls.

"Now, I know you got some mad hotties in your class, do tell," Jason said, lightly smacking me in the arm.

"Eww. That's sick man. What you gonna do, rob the cradle?" Jarek asked, given that I was in 8th grade, and they were in 10th.

"At least I don't dress like a bible salesman." Jason said to Jarek with a chuckle.

"Hey, it's not his fault his grandma dresses him," Ethan said, laughing.

"Dude, whose side are you on?" Jarek asked, smacking Ethan on the arm.

I looked forward to the next year when I'd be at the same school as these guys.

"So whhaatt you you you got that for?" Darnel asked Jarek, pointing to the New Liberator he was still holding.

"Ah shit, don't ask. Jarek's obsessed with that rag, like an Enquirer for people who live in the Colorado mountains." Ethan said.

"Come on. It is not an Enquirer. It's totally vetted, cited. See here," he said, gesturing to citations at the end of the article he'd been reading earlier.

"Uh-huh," Ethan said, rolling his eyes.

"Let me see," Jason said, taking the paper out of Jarek's hand and looking it over.

"Nahh, no, I-I . . . my mmmm . . . Mom's ex-boyf-fr-friend, D-da-David, used to read that thing always." Darnel said.

"I don't know. Sounds like bullshit, but I will say my dad works at the hospital and he's a complete douche, so . . ." Jason said, trailing off.

David? David! I thought as a lightbulb went off in my head. Ethan stood near with my alphabet chart waving in his right hand as my thoughts drifted to what I wanted to say, tuning out the rest of their chatter. I imagined I'd casually walk to him, taking the board and spelling out, 'Hey, I know David' but this ol' body of mine hunched over, continually tapping the pencil Ethan had given me earlier. I meandered my way to Ethan's side, as I thought of taking the board. My hand flailed and all I could do was squeeze his arm.

"Hey man. What's up?" Ethan asked, aggressively pulling his arm away, while I lunged forward, grabbing his arm again.

"Ha! Rock n' Roll! A little get up and go. I like your umphf, man!" Jason said, strongly gripping my shoulder, giving a shake and knocking me out of my trance.

"We need to get going anyhow," Ethan said as he swiftly moved in the direction to go downhill.

"See if he wants to say something," Jarek said, with his nose still in the paper.

"What? Oh, right." Ethan said, then lifting the board to my eyeline, he handed me a pencil.

"Why the pencil?" Jason asked.

"Huh? I don't know, he's just more accurate that way." Ethan said. "So, what is it, dick?"

'D,A,V,I,D' I spelled.

"Ddd-David, that's my m-m-Mom's ex." Darnel said.

"Yeah, we just heard you, dumass," Jason said.

"Go on, Michael, what about him?" Ethan asked.

'I, K,N,O,W, H,I,N,' Shit, I thought: I meant 'M'.

"You know him? How?" Ethan asked.

"T,H,E,J,H,E,B,A,L,T,H,S,T,O,R.E,' So many typos, I hoped he'd u nderstand.

"The store? The health store?" Ethan asked as I felt the pressure to get out what I wanted to say, knowing that they were growing bored with my slow pace.

"That place Mom sends me on the bus to buy her flour? That place sucks!" Ethan said.

"Y-y-yeah, that's where he w-w-works." Darnel said.

"Oh, alright, so you've met him, that's cool," Ethan said, shifting again, restless, and ready to head down the hill. "Well, it's been real. It's been fun, but it hasn't been real fun."

"Later," Jason said, as they all exchanged the s'up bro head acknowledgement. "Go tell Sam, I said 'hi,' *la la la*" he continued, making a gesture with his tongue.

"You're a degenerate." Ethan said, jibbing.

"Yeah, I know," Jason said, shrugging his shoulders in a 'what ya gonna do' manner.

Ethan started down the hill, right when my body went stiff. He walked for several beats before realizing I hadn't moved.

"Ah shit. Not this again," Ethan said, begrudgingly heading towards me.

Jarek folded the paper under his arm, then headed towards Ethan. "Gimme that," he said, snatching the alphabet board out of Ethan's hand, heading over to me.

"What's up, man?" He asked, picking the pencil up off the ground, then placing the board in front of me.

'D,A,V,I,D, G,A,V,E, M,O,M' I spelled, then took the pencil and started flicking it.

Snatching the pencil out of my hand, then handing it back to me, Jarek said, "David gave Mom what?"

'T,H,E, P,A,P,E,R', I spelled.

"The paper?" Jarek asked, puzzled as I thought, 'Damn, I knew I should have spelled out the entire name.'

"This paper." Ethan said, yanking the paper from where Jarek was holding it under his arm. "He must be talking about this."

"Is that it?" Jarek asked.

'Y,E,S,' I spelled.

Chapter 15

GINO'S PIZZA!

Afterschool one afternoon, Jarek and Ethan were rummaging through the fridge looking for food.

"Your mom doesn't give, you shit. There's no chips, no hot pockets, no microwaveable pizzas. What's in this?" He said, pulling out a Chinese food container. "Ahh, nasty. Smell that!"

"Ah bro, I believe you. You don't have to shove it in my face." Ethan said, pushing the box away, then dumping it into the trash.

"Well, now what? I need something more substantial than convenience store, chips, and dips." Jarek said.

"How about we go to your house and have grams cook for us?" Ethan asked.

Ethan rarely went to Jarek's house, but had spent the night a few times. I had never been, but was curious to meet his family.

"Nah, I don't want to go there," Jarek said.

"Why not?" Ethan asked.

"Because I don't. Let me see how much money I have," he said, rummaging through his backpack.

"I've probably got some change for the arcade. Let me check." Ethan said, rummaging through the junk drawer collecting quarters.

"I have almost 10 bucks. That should be enough for me, and you broke ass bitches." Jarek said, shoving the money into his front pocket as we collected ourselves and headed out the door.

This was the first time I'd been to Gino's.

One thing easy to miss about San Francisco was the food. If you had a hankering for French, Vietnamese, Italian or exotic Thai, it could be delivered day or night from any number of 5-star restaurants, not that Mom let us have any of it. Here, if you wanted delivery, there was Gino's pizza or Lucky House Chinese. We ate there all the time, but I had never been inside either of them.

Gino's was smaller than I expected, given how much everyone frequented there. It was white all over, including the tables except the red chairs and the stained glass lamps. The walls were embossed with high school paraphernalia, a pennant reading 'Class of '86', a football jersey in a glass case, number 8 Morello, and many artifacts from the year 1986. The arcade, if you could call it that, was two games, Tron, and Ms. Pac-man.

"Hey where is everybody?" Jarek asked, noticing the quiet surroundings.

"They're at the football game," a voice said, coming from behind.

We turned around to notice a tall, thin man with waist length hair, held back in a ponytail. He was wearing a white apron covered in tomato sauce and his glow was a greenish/blue.

"You didn't hear?" He asked. "There's a game tonight. On game nights, there's no crowd until after the game."

"Oh, I guess we didn't hear," Jarek said, embarrassed.

"What do you want?" He asked, moving around the counter.

"We'll take a pizza." Jarek said.

"No shit. Size? Toppings?" The Man asked.

"Oh yeah, right. I only have ten bucks, so like 3 slices I guess." Jarek said.

"You're spotting the whole crew here?" He asked, gesturing towards me and Ethan.

"Yeah, I guess." Jarek said with a shrug.

"That's decent of you," he said, yanking the ten dollars out of Jarek's hand, examining it by the light with a smirk, put it inside the cash register. "Hey, how about you get a large one topping?"

"I don't think that's enough," Jarek said.

"It's fine. What do you want?" He asked.

The door flung open and a voice from behind said, "Hey Tony, I ran into your ex-luuva at the store today. She's says..."

We turned around to see a tall young man in his 20s. His neck length light brown hair shined with blondish highlights in the light, his glow reminded me of the eye color hazel, in some lights it was greenish then occasionally it might look light brown but not in an ominous way more in a woodsy way, like he was the kind of guy who could live in a tree. I'd noticed this woodsy glow before. It was David, the very one we had been talking about that afternoon on Kite-Hill.

"I didn't think there'd be anyone in here yet. What's up, fellas?" David said, glancing at us with a bright array of shiny white teeth, then quickly making a double take back at me. "I know you. You're uh . . . hmm . . . don't tell me it'll come to me."

Darting over, he sat down, taking off his jean jacket revealing the wool interior. A copy of the New Liberator popped out from the inside of his jacket pocket.

"That's Michael." Jarek said.

"Michael? Michael. Yeah, pumpkin smoothie, right? You don't come in with your mom anymore. Have a seat, gentlemen." David said, gesturing for us to take a seat across from him.

"Hey kid, what do you say, pepperoni?" Tony asked.

"Yeah, that's great." Jarek said with a smile. "Thanks again, man."

Jarek and Ethan took a seat while I stood bopping a straw I'd picked up from the counter. "Hey, Michael, sit down." Ethan said, pulling a chair out for me to sit next to him.

All three of us on one side, David on the other with his jacket in a seat of its own, looked at the large pepperoni heading our way that Tony was carrying. Sliding it on the table, he plopped down a stack of white paper plates, then returned with a pitcher of ice water, taking another chair, and turning it around backwards as he sat with his legs straddled on either side of the chair. Reaching out, I took a gentle squeeze on Tony's arm; he had such a warm glow I felt compelled to d o so.

Unphased by my gesture, he gave my hand a little tap, without even looking over, then with the other arm gestured for everyone to take their slice. "Eat up fellas!" He said, leaning back grabbing a parmesan shaker from another table.

Noticing a few loose strains of hair on his shirt, I picked them off, releasing them to the floor. "Thanks man, I guess I need my hairnet." Tony said.

"Hey, you have a copy of the New Liberator." Jarek said, gesturing to the newspaper poking out of David's jacket as he grabbed a slice and popped it in his mouth.

Noticing I wasn't reaching for a slice, Tony took one and put it on a plate for me. "Here, the best one in the pie. Eat up, kid."

"Yeah, you know about this?" David asked with a smirk.

"He's obsessed with it." Ethan said, shoveling a slice into his mouth.

"Totally get that, man. It's good stuff. We know who writes it." David casually added.

"No, we don't," Tony said.

"You know who writes this?" Jarek asked with wide eyes.

"No, he doesn't know shit." Tony said.

"Come on, it's gotta be her." David said.

"Ahh," Tony said, brushing his statement off, then stood up and walked back into the kitchen.

"Don't listen to him." David said, as Tony returned with a stack of cups, sitting backwards on his chair.

"Liz is crazy, but she's not that crazy. Some of the stuff in there is too out there, even for her." Tony said.

"Hey, you must be the one who gave my mom the newspaper. You work at Country Life, right?" Ethan asked.

"Yeah, that's right. For now, I work there until I get my book published." David said.

"What book?" Tony asked.

"Never mind," David said.

"Oh right. I remember. Darnel said you used to date his mom." Jarek said.

"Who's Darnel? Oh, Darnel. Little guy. Yeah, I remember him. His Mom was hot. I like older caramel women." David said with a wink as he leaned back in his chair.

"Sure, you like 'em short, tall, blondes, brunettes, redheads, straight hair, long hair..." Tony said.

"Fat ones, skinny ones, ones who climb on rocks," David said with a smirk.

"Anyway, staff should be here any minute." Tony said, looking at his watch, then getting up, he grabbed another slice and plopped it down on my plate. "Second best slice. Eat up fellas, then get out; I've got a crowd coming in about 10." He continued, disappearing into the kitchen.

"Don't mind him. He's still bitter." David said.

"What do you know about who wrote it?" Jarek asked.

"She used to be a nurse at the hospital and saw some effed-up stuff." David said.

"That's enough," Tony shouted from inside the kitchen.

"Ah, man, I knew this shit was real." Jarek said.

"How does that prove it real?" Ethan asked.

"Oh, it's real." David said.

"If it's real, then why can't someone go to the police?" Ethan said, grabbing the copy out of Jarek's backpack, then sliding it across the table. "A girl has been essentially sold by her drug-addicted parents to science. I mean, this can't be legal."

"You'd be surprised what's considered to be 'legal'. That's an old copy. Let me give you mine. I'm finished with it," he said, taking the newspaper from his jacket pocket and sliding it across the table to Jarek.

"We know that one article is real, so why not..." Jarek said.

"Which article?" David asked.

"The one about the fake blood. Their mom works at the big building and..." Jarek started when Ethan slid his foot under the table, kicking Jarek.

"Your mom works there? Then you can get in. I've been trying to find a way to get in since they erected that monstrosity. You gotta get in there, guys, verify some of this stuff, or even get some new intel," David said.

"The only one who's ever been there is Michael." Jarek said.

"Well, Michael, it's up to you man." David said, throwing another slice of pizza on my plate.

"So, if all this true, then why? What's the end goal here?" Ethan asked.

"You ever hear of the eugenics movement?" David asked.

"Like Nazis and shit?" Jarek asked.

"Yeah, exactly." David said.

"So, there's Nazis in Jukeville?" Ethan asked sarcastically.

"Sort of... well, no, not exactly. Not the way you might think. They don't target race or creed anymore. They're obsessed with genetics. They want only the 'fittest' in society, but no one is perfect, so they have to . . . create it. No, that's not the right word..." David said.

"Manufacture it?" Ethan asked.

"Yeah, that's it." David said.

"The master race. This is some Nazi shit." Jarek said.

"But what about, like, government oversight? It can't be like this big thing that everyone is in on. That's ridiculous." Ethan said.

"Well, it's complicated. You know the Cold War, that they say we're no longer in, but I have my doubts. Anyway, it's like that inside the government." David said.

"What does that even mean?" Ethan asked.

"It's like America has spies, right? Russia has spies. The Russian spies pretend to be American; the American spies pretend to be Russian. Then some will defect, so you have an American pretending to be Russian spying on Russians (who is now with the Russians for real), then starts spying on the Americans. Meanwhile, the Russians are doing the same thing in reverse. You, see?" David said.

"Wait, what? That doesn't make any sense. Who works for who?" Ethan asked.

"Exactly." David said.

Then, like an avalanche, the place became flooded with teens. The chatter was incessant, and the screaming was a bullet in my ear. I stood up, taking my straw from the table, and began tapping once more.

"I guess that's our cue." Ethan said, standing up, as we gathered our things and navigated our way through the sea of teens, heading for the door.

Outside, Ethan stopped to put on his jacket and backpack.

"That guy's full of shit," Ethan said.

"I don't know, sounds legit to me." Jarek said.

"Dude, if that's true and there's no one to turn to, we're screwed." Ethan said, pointing back at the restaurant as if David were standing there.

"Well, maybe it's up to us." Jarek said.

"Well, may the almighty flying spaghetti monster have mercy on us all." Ethan said with a chuckle.

Chapter 16

HALLOWEEN 1993

One afternoon, heading to pick up Alyssa, Jarek noticed a station wagon with tinted windows.

"Family cars used to abduct suspects, whistle blowers and even children used in genetic engineering experiments," Jarek said, reading from the New Liberator.

"See how ridiculous that is, I mean, family cars in the suburbs. Shocker!" Ethan said.

Even after spotting it several times throughout the week in multiple locations, Ethan remained a skeptic, but on Sunday, Halloween of all days, when it appeared parked in front of our house, he changed his t
une.

"Hey, Mom, do you know who owns that station wagon?" Ethan asked, peering through the blinds.

"Station wagon?" Mom asked, looking through the blinds. "It probably belongs to an out-of-town visitor."

"Yeah, that's what I'm afraid of," Ethan whispered as Mom buzzed away in response to Alyssa's cries for help with her costume.

She wore her 'Good Witch' costume to the school's Halloween parade on Friday, which she couldn't stop going on about. "I mean, it was the best, Mom. You should have seen Laura's costume, which was almost as same as mine but like a little different color, cause you know how mine is purplish. She was like totally black, maybe like a little purple but mostly black."

I was glad she found it fun, as I remembered those being walks around the schoolyard in a hot, itchy costume.

"I'm sorry honey, you know I wish I could have been there too." Mom said.

I never enjoyed trick-or-treating either and when Mom asked me if I wanted to go this year, I spelled out a definite 'N,O'. This was going to be a problem, as Ethan was planning to go to a party at Jason's house and Alyssa had her heart absolutely set on trick-or-treating.

Ethan and Jarek were getting ready, too. Ethan needed Mom's help with the make-up as he was going as Arnold Schwarzenegger from Terminator 2. You know, the part where half his face is gone, and he has the creepy cyborg eye. Mom did a stellar job; his face was truly grotesque. Jarek had a Freddy Krueger mask with the knife glove and the whole works. I didn't have a costume and told everyone I didn't want one but much to my surprise Ethan borrowed a Public Enemy t-shirt from Darnel and said all I needed was the shirt, a flannel to go over it, jeans, and some tennis shoes to be John Connor from Terminator 2. It was so much more comfortable than other costumes, besides it was kind of nice being included.

After we were dressed; Mom was so excited that she had us stand together and take pictures. She must have taken a dozen already, when she said, "Just one more." Then said it again, and again, and again...

Alyssa fed up, whined, "Come on, let's go!" And grabbed Mom's hand.

I so badly didn't wish to go that I froze and wouldn't move.

"Come on, Michael," Alyssa said, walking over and grabbing my hand.

Standing stiff, flicking my fingers in my face, Alyssa complained, "Mom, can we just go?"

"Michael needs to come with us," Mom said.

"He can come with us." Jarek said.

"I'm okay with it. I mean, we're both Terminator 2 costumes. We should stick together." Ethan said, giving me a punch in the arm.

"Are you sure?" Mom asked.

"Yeah, no big deal. He's with me all the time, anyway." Ethan said.

"We'll look after him, Mrs. Hogan. There's nothing to worry about." Jarek said.

"You guys aren't going to drink or anything, you promise?" Mom asked.

"Mom, come on, I don't do that, just go. Alyssa's losing her mind." Ethan said.

And just like that, I was invited to my first party. I could hardly believe my excitement. I flapped and flicked like nobody's business. I had never been to Jason's house before, nor any friend's house for that matter.

It was getting dark when I realized we had been walking in circles for over an hour. I kept taking Ethan's arm, wrapping mine around it, even when he pulled away. Jarek and Ethan stopped a couple times to trick-or-treat for candy while I waited. If anyone asked if I wanted some also, they always said 'yes', but I refused to eat it, letting them keep it for themselves.

"Didn't you say you've been to Jason's house before?" Ethan asked.

"Yes, it's around here. I know it's on..." Jarek said.

"Sierra Vista Drive, I know, you've said that." Ethan said.

As the night crept in, bringing the autumn chill, fewer and fewer children lined the streets. The aroma of burnt pumpkins filled the air, as the candle in the jack-o'-lanterns burned to the nub.

"Maybe we should call it a night." Ethan said.

"No, let's keep going, just no more stopping. We're almost there." Jarek said.

While trudging along, they began a discussion about the ridiculous predictability of horror films. Personally, I don't understand why people think blood splattering is entertainment. Then Jarek abruptly stopped, reaching his arms out for us to stop as well.

"Hey, has that station wagon been there this whole time?" Jarek asked.

"Where?" Ethan asked, turning around to look.

"Don't be so obvious." Jarek said.

I noticed it a couple times, but no one brought my alphabet board.

"Hey, let's get outta here." Ethan said.

It moved slowly as Jarek tapped my arm, urging me to speed up. It continued inching steadily closer, as if at the same speed as us. I started laughing, almost toppling over when Jarek grabbed my shirt, instructing me to keep going. Once Ethan and Jarek started running, I tried to keep up as the station wagon moved behind us. Jarek took a turn down the next street and we followed; the vehicle right behind us. Ethan noticed an alley behind a row of single-story apartments, too narrow to drive, so we ran through it, attempting to lose our stalker. The station wagon parked directly in front of the alley when Jarek spotted a slightly ajar red door. He opened it and went in as we followed.

The place savored of candle wax and lavender or maybe jasmine, whatever those oils were that Mom put on my pillow to help me sleep. The room was dim, barely lit with candles and oil burning lamps. I tried blowing some out, but Ethan stopped me. Like an indoor jungle, plants were everywhere, including a large tower of fragrant herbs.

"Let's see if there's a phone." Jarek said, tiptoeing.

"We should get out of here." Ethan said.

"And do what? Go back out there while Michael Meyers waits to kill us?" Jarek asked.

"Maybe we're just being paranoid, we don't know," Ethan said, before going mute noticing a woman in the kitchen.

She had on headphones with her back turned to us. On the counter, there was an odd contraption, something you'd be more likely to see in a science lab than a home kitchen, possibly a distillery. Stunned, she turned around to find us standing there.

"What are you guys doing in my house?" She said with a start, as she pulled a Glock from behind her back.

When she aimed the gun at us, Ethan and Jarek raised their hands like the people do in the movies. I laughed and flapped my arms; noticing me, the woman's face softened. Continuing to stare, she gave me a look like she was trying to remember where she knew me, as her gun slowly came down.

"I hope you are trick-or-treaters and not murderers," she said, putting the Glock on the counter and grabbing a bowl.

Extending the bowl towards us, the candy inside looked vaguely like the kind Mom made for me each Halloween.

"Sorry we were running from..." Jarek started to explain when Ethan smacked his shoulder, giving him a look.

"I thought the trick-or-treaters were gone, so I started working and listening to my books on tape. I didn't hear a knock. Was my door open?" The woman asked.

"Yes, that red door from the alley." Jarek said, pointing to the door.

"What are you guys thinking, coming into a person's house on Halloween night, wearing serial killer masks on your head?" She asked, gesturing to Jarek's Freddy Krueger mask.

"Oh, right," Jarek said, taking it off.

"Hey, don't I know you?" The woman asked, recognizing Jarek.

Jarek stumbled a little while, shaking his head. "Uh, I don't, I don't know..."

"Your father is Mr. Williams, Eldrian Williams. Right?" She asked.

"Yeah, I mean, that's my grandfather. How do you know gramps?" Jarek asked.

"I used to come to your house and do physical therapy with him," she said.

"Oh, yeah, I remember you. You taught him how to use the alphabet board." Jarek said with a sigh of relief and a note of recognition.

"You're the one who did that? My mom has been interested in meeting you." Ethan said.

"Really? Well, she's welcome to come by." The woman said, walking into another room.

It was too dark to see anything, as we reluctantly followed the sound of her voice. Lighting a large oil lamp and a few candles, I could see that she had converted her living room into a store. There were bookshelves filled with jars, bottles, and tinctures. On top of one of the bookshelves there was a scale and a container of empty vitamin capsules. Dozens of books, like the kind Mom always read on nutrition, health, and topics like that, were everywhere. As she lit more candles, I could see there was a massage table up against one wall and another side of the room revealed an old, antique rocking chair. Tired from all the walking, I went over to the chair to sit down. Noticing I wanted to sit, she came over, removing the knitting needles and yarn that were placed on the seat, moving them to her desk, which stood near the front of the door. Unlike Dr. Cody's desk, hers was tidy and minimalist, with no more than an Aloe Vera plant, business cards, a clipboard, a cup of pens, a calculator, and an antique cash register.

"Sorry, it's dark in here. I don't use electricity if I can help it," she said.

"Can I get your phone number or something so my mom can contact you?" Ethan asked.

"Of course." She said, picking up a card from her desk.

Handing the card to Ethan, I peeked through my peripheral to see what it said. Adorned with a beautiful vine that snaked around the trim, the center read: Lizzy Kinney, PT, RN, MH followed by a phone number.

Sitting down at her desk, Lizzy looked over and asked once again, "So, are you going to tell me what you were thinking entering a stranger's house on Halloween night?"

Jarek and Ethan looked at each other, not knowing what to say, remaining quiet for a long time.

Pointing at Jarek, Lizzy began, "You started saying you were running from someone. Or something."

"There was a car that looked like it was following us," Jarek said.

"We were probably just being paranoid." Ethan said.

"Car? What kind of car? Was it a station wagon?" Lizzy asked.

Hearing that, I started flickering my fingers in my face and making a loud sound. Everyone looked over as Lizzy got up, handing me another one of her homemade candies, then sitting down at the desk, noting the look of surprise on Ethan and Jarek's faces.

"It was, wasn't it?" She asked.

"How did you know?" Jarek asked.

"I'll be. Because it's been following me for months," she said.

"Following you? It's been following us for several days." Jarek said.

"Why would a station wagon be following you?" Ethan asked Lizzy.

"I really can't say, I just know that this town . . . well, it's changed since the big building," she began, before taking a pause.

"What about this town?" Jarek asked.

"I came here to do my residency at that hospital ten years ago. I loved my work. I helped people and thought I'd never leave, but then about three years ago when that building got erected. I don't know, things started to change. I didn't like the direction things were going, so I left and never looked back. I'm still a nurse and a PT but I won't do it in that environment." She said.

"What did you see there?" Jarek asked.

"Things that some people might not want to get out." Lizzy said.

"Things that might get someone followed?" Jarek asked.

"That's what it looks like." Lizzy said.

"I KNEW IT! I knew it, didn't I tell you guys? This place is shady." Jarek said.

Lizzy got up and went into the kitchen to grab her Glock. Placing her gun in the back of her pants and covering it with her shirt, she looked out the window.

"I don't see it out front." She said.

"Last we saw it; it was following us back there." Ethan said, pointing to the red door we came through.

"I can't believe I left that door open; I always keep it locked." Lizzy said, heading towards it. She walked outside and looked around, then came back in, locking the door behind her. "Okay, there's no one out there now. Do you guys need a ride somewhere?"

"Should we still try to get to Jason's party? I mean, I feel bad if we don't." Jarek said.

"Are you crazy? It's Halloween. We had a gun pulled on us, no offense." Ethan said, pivoting towards Lizzy. "It's late and we have a psycho stalker following us. No, we're going home."

I was a little disappointed to be missing my first party, but I had to say I agreed. It was late, plus I was cold and scared. Lizzy grabbed her keys and a coat that was hanging on a rack near the front door.

Ethan and Jarek stood behind her but, I sat in the chair flicking my fingers while rocking. "Come on, Michael," Lizzy said, as I got up and walked over to where they were waiting.

"Did we tell you our names?" Ethan asked.

"Uhm. What do you mean?" She asked.

"You said, 'Michael,' how did you know my brother's name?" Ethan asked.

"Uh, one of you guys said it." Lizzy said.

Ethan didn't say anything more, and we all looked at each other, as if to say, 'what a night.'

Chapter 17

JASON'S PARTY THE AFTERMATH

When we got home Halloween night, Mom was waiting up. Ethan told her how we met Lizzy while trick- or-treating and gave Mom her card. It surprised me he said nothing else about what happened that night. Alyssa was already asleep, and Mom looked tired. She told us to turn our clocks back for daylight savings and go to bed.

The next day afterschool, Ethan and Jarek were waiting in the driveway as usual. They told me to go in the house, use the restroom and that we had to visit Jason at the hospital. I didn't like the sound of that, as the last time I was at the hospital was when Dad died.

On the walk there, I expected us to talk about the night before. Everything that happened with Lizzy and the station wagon had been racing in my mind all night, but they barely mentioned it. They were preoccupied by the news about a famous actor not much older than us who had died early on Halloween morning.

"It's weird, no?" Jarek said.

"Which part?" Ethan asked.

"I don't know, all of it. The *Stand Buy Me* guy dies, Jason, our night... Like a cursed night." Jarek said.

First thing I noticed upon arrival at the hospital was that sterile stench of ammonia and the white walls that make you feel like they're closing in on you. I took Ethan's arm and gave it a squeeze with my chin.

"Dude, we need to hang in there. Chill," Ethan said.

Jarek headed to the counter at the front desk and asked the clerk for Jason's room.

"Jason Greene, you say?" The Clerk asked.

"Yes." Jarek said.

Looking back at her computer, she said, "Give me a minute."

She was speaking to another nurse who looked familiar, and I wondered if it was Nurse Delores. I took Ethan's arm again, pressing my chin deep into it.

Pulling away, he insisted, "Come on, can't you hang in there for just a bit, we're trying to see Jason."

I knew they wanted me to calm down, and I desperately wanted to please them.

Looking around, I saw the fish tank I noticed the last time. As I started walking towards it, a large group of residents came through. They were enveloped in their conversation. While not regarding me at all, they walked right past. Getting turned around, unsure where I was, I tried heading back to Ethan, flickering my fingers in my face, but before I knew it, I found myself wandering into the elevator. The others in the lift gawked in my direction, as if they knew I didn't belong there, but no one said a word.

Time went by as the elevator dinged with each coming and going, but no Ethan. Finally, alone in the elevator, things went black, as the lift abruptly ceased.

The sound of a shrill siren awakened the elevator with a jolt as the light returned, reigniting its ascension. Then a ding followed as the doors opened. Looking up, I could see the number 13 was lit.

There was no one outside waiting, and the floor appeared empty. The doors remained open for what felt like a long while, so I exited.

There were no people walking the halls, but there were patients in the rooms. The first was sizeable with 30 or so people, both men and women, naked, laying on narrow slabs with their limbs hanging over the side. Cords were inserted into various parts of the body, including the head, leading up to, I don't know where. I couldn't tell if they were living or dead, if the cords were strapped around them or inside them somehow. Dangling there partially suspended by the lines, there were these black wires underneath, leading to what looked like a generator. I half thought for a second that I was watching one of Ethan and Jarek's horror films, only much creepier. Jarred I flapped backwards and continued down the hall.

Noticing a room with a pink door and walls ordained with the children's fairytale scene of *Hansel & Gretel*, I thought it might be a good place to find a friendly face. Inside there was a little bald girl, around Alyssa's age, sitting there alone on the floor with electrodes stuck to her head. I wanted to go inside, but investigating further, I spotted the man with the brown glow. Startled, I raced down the hall, making noises. Men and women in scrubs started coming out of the rooms to see what the commotion was, including the man with the brown glow. Terrified, I panicked. As I felt myself going into a full meltdown, I was in front of the elevator again. When the doors opened, a nurse reached out, taking me by the hand pulling me back into the lift.

"Your brother is looking for you. Don't worry, I'll take you to him," she said as the doors shut behind us and we descended to the main floor. Upon our arrival, Ethan and Jarek were waiting.

"You gave me a heart attack." Ethan said.

"Well, we got him now. Let's just go to Jason's room." Jarek said.

When we got to floor three, Ethan grabbed my jacket and directed me to get off the lift.

"Stay with me!" He insisted as we walked to room 313.

Jason was lying in the bed, not looking so great. He had a wrap around his head, his legs, and his right arm.

"Hey guys," Jason said enthusiastically as he saw us.

"Hey, how you feeling?" Jarek asked.

"Ah, I'm okay. Just banged up, being stupid. What's up with you guys? You look like shit." Jason said gesturing towards Ethan.

"Oh, just this guy," Ethan said, punching me in the arm. "This guy took off on us and we had to look all over the hospital. We would have been here much sooner."

"Ah, he probably just thinks this place sucks balls like I do." Jason said, then looking at me added, "I want to get the hell out of here too, man."

"So, what happened?" Jarek asked.

"I should ask you the same thing. Why didn't you guys make it last night?" Jason asked.

"We got lost and then it got really late, so we decided to go home." Ethan said.

"We were freaked the hell out last night..." Jarek said.

"Ah, you guys were scared little girls on Halloween night," Jason said.

"Yeah, I guess you could say that." Ethan said. Jarek got the hint and said no more.

"You gonna tell us what happened or not?" Ethan asked.

"Not! Nah, it was stupid. I got wasted on my dad's stash and went to the roof." Jason said.

"Ah, man," Jarek said, getting squeamish.

"Broke my leg, my ankle, my arm and cracked my head open." Jason said.

"Eww, dude, what the hell you doing on the roof?" Jarek said.

"I don't know," Jason said.

"Well, maybe girls will find the cast sexy." Ethan said.

"Ah, shut up," Jason said, chuckling.

A nurse came in and told us visiting hours were over.

"When are you going home?" Jarek asked as we were being ushered out.

"I think in a day or two. Maybe you guys can come to the house. I know I'm about to be bored as shit." Jason said.

"Alright man, we'll see you soon then." Ethan said, as we continued our way out of the hospital. Following the hospital, we picked up Alyssa and went home. In the basement, Jarek questioned Ethan about why he didn't want to tell Jason the Lizzy and station wagon story.

"I didn't want to freak him out. We're supposed to tell him that we think my dad was murdered in the very hospital he's in. I mean, why would I want to do that to him?" Ethan asked.

"I see your point." Jarek said.

"I prefer we just keep it between us." Ethan said.

I wanted to tell them about the 13th floor, how I saw the people with cords, the girl with the electrodes and the brown man. So, I walked over to the ABC chart on the wall and started tapping.

"You want to say something?" Jarek asked, gesturing for me to come over and sit on the couch. "Come on."

I sat next to him while he pulled the 8x10 alphabet chart and a pen from his backpack.

"Yeah, I'd like to know what the hell happened when you took off on us." Ethan said.

"Go ahead," Jarek said, holding the chart and handing me the pen.

Not sure where to begin, I started spelling out 'T,H,I,R,T,E,E,N,T,H.'

"Yeah, that's where the nurse found you the 13th floor. What about it?" Jarek asked.

Feeling put on the spot, I started to mess up, 'S,T, then S,T again. Jarek moved the chart away and brought it back.

"Did you see anything on the 13th floor?" He asked.

'Y,E,S.' I spelled.

"What?" Jarek asked.

'A, G,I,R,L' I spelled.

"A girl? What's with the girl?" He asked.

'T,H,E, B,R,O,W,N, M,A,N' I spelled.

"What's the brown man?" Ethan asked. 'H,E, K,I,L,L,E,D, D,A,D' I spelled.

Ethan and Jarek went silent. I don't know why I said that it was a strong feeling that came over me.

Chapter 18

THE RETURN OF THE MAN WITH THE BROWN GLOW

The next afternoon, Jarek and Ethan took me to Jason's house since he was discharged from the hospital. His family was one of the wealthiest in town and had an enormous house. The walkway was ornate with flowers and expensive art. I had never seen a house with its own private pool nor such a large dining room table. They kept their dishes in glass cases so you could see them rather than hidden in cabinets.

Darnel was also there and told us in private, before we saw Jason, that he had gone up to the roof to jump into his own pool when he hit the side before falling into the water. He was drunk and trying to impress his party guests. It made me think the lengths people go to be liked says a lot about our need for connection.

Jason's room was upstairs and was nothing like the rest of the house. Rock posters of Nirvana, Black Sabbath, and Metallica, as well as girls in bikinis or less, covered the walls. It was dark, with black curtains and a black carpet. His bed was made up like the one in the hospital, so he could use a remote control to lift himself up. There was a woman who came in and took away dirty dishes while offering to bring more food; he didn't want any.

I could sense Jason's mood was different than what it had been at the hospital. There, aside from the broken bones, he looked normal, but today he was lethargic.

"Thaankss for coming byyy," Jason said.

Noticeably, Ethan and Jarek were disturbed by the change as well.

"Yeah, of course we were glad to hear you were out of the hospital so soon." Ethan said.

"Too soon, fatther says, I may neeeddd to go... to back." Jason said, as his slurs got worse.

"Well, that sucks." Jarek said.

"I'm feeelin' tired now." Jason said, then turned over.

The lady, (presumably a nurse) came in and pulled the blankets to cover Jason, then motioned for us to leave.

"Alright, feel better." Jarek said, while Darnel walked us out. Once we left the house, he took us aside to talk.

"Hey, has he been like this all day?" Jarek asked Darnel.

"I came just before you guys, so as long as I've been here." Darnel said.

Darnel's stutter was gone.

"We should give him some time. I mean, he just fell off a roof. I'm sure he's a little messed up right now, but he'll be back to normal in a few weeks, maybe a month." Ethan said.

"It's weird though, right? I mean, he was fine at the hospital." Jarek said.

"Maybe it's the pain meds." Ethan said.

"Yeah, but wasn't he on pain meds at the hospital, too?" Darnel asked.

"I don't know. Maybe they upped the dose. We'll have to be patient. It's only been a couple days since he fell off a roof. It's amazing he's alive." Ethan said.

A polished, clean, expensive looking silver Mercedes pulled up the driveway. I recognized the driver right away; he was the man from the hospital with the brown glow. As he stalked towards us, I grabbed Ethan's arm and jabbed my chin into it. His appearance was as I remembered: freshly cut hair, fancy suit and shiny shoes that made a clackety clack with each step he took. Ethan ignored me, so I started to jab harder and even opened my mouth to press my teeth on his arm.

"Hey, relax dude, we're leaving in a minute." Ethan said.

Smiling as he approached, I could see he recognized me, then his smile disappeared.

"Hello gentlemen, are you here to see Jason?" He asked.

"Yes, we just saw him." Jarek said.

Yanking Ethan by the arm, I almost pulled him down to the ground. Breaking his arm away, he told me again to 'chill'.

"We were just leaving." Ethan said.

The man with the brown glow didn't say anything about how he knew me, despite looking over at me several times. He examined my melting down like he was trying to compute or was taking data.

"Are you leaving as well, Darnel? I can give you a lift home if you want to stay for dinner." The Man with the Brown Glow asked.

"Sure, Dr. Greene, I can hang out a little longer." Darnel said.

"It was nice meeting you," he said to the rest of us as he put his hand on Darnel's shoulder and directed him back inside the house.

Though I had calmed by now, when we arrived at the end of the block, Ethan turned to me, punching me in the arm.

"I'm so sick of you starting shit when we go places. Can't you get it together?" Ethan asked.

"Come on, man, he can't help it. He's trying." Jarek said.

Hurt, I began whining and even crying a little while plopping myself on the ground, rocking back and forth.

"See, you made it worse." Jarek said.

"You sound like my mom." Ethan said.

Kneeling next to me and pulling the alphabet chart out of his backpack, Jarek asked, "What's up, man? You hungry?"

'Y,E,S' I spelled.

"Okay, let's get some food then." Jarek said, as he put the chart in his backpack.

Refusing to get up, I whined louder, when Jarek pulled the chart back out and asked, "Is it something else?"

'Y,E,S', I spelled.

"What?" He asked.

"D,R, G,R,E,E,N,E,' I spelled.

"Jason's father?" Jarek asked.

'Y,E,S', I spelled.

"What about him?" Ethan asked.

'H,E,S, T,H,E,' I spelled, then started to miss-poke, so Jarek took the chart away and asked again.

"He's the_____?" Jarek asked, bringing the chart in front of me.

'B,R,O,W,N, M,A,N,' I spelled.

Chapter 19

BOYS NIGHT OUT

It was Friday night. Alyssa was having a sleep-over at a friend's house, Mom was at her grief support group, and Jarek was staying with us. Down in the basement, we were bored.

Looking for something on the radio, Ethan switched from station to station, where every other channel was playing "I Will Always Love You" covered by Whitney Houston. Intermittently we'd hear "Jump Around" by House of Pain, a few seconds of "Smells Like Teen Spirit", then "Mysterious Ways" by U2 and back to "I Will Always Love You".

Ethan's impatience with the radio reminded me of Dad. One classic rock station picked up "The Pinball Wizard" by the WHO, which took me back to a day Dad brought me to the beach. The two of us drove for hours, listening to music with the window rolled all the way down. I didn't know where the rest of the family was or what they were doing that day. All I knew was that it was me and Dad doing our thing. His cigarette smoke swirled and swished in a quick whip before blowing out the window.

He asked, "Do you hear that?"

Then took my hand and taught me how to drum on my leg. I'd hit so hard that it would leave a handprint on my upper thigh, but I didn't care.

"Keith Moon is the man. You feel that energy?" He asked.

I smiled, moving from side to side as he took my hand again, showing me how to slap my thigh, keeping time with the beat.

"Yeah, that's it, you got it," he said, singing along, though he rarely got the lyrics right.

Back in the basement, Ethan switched stations once more. "I Will Always Love You" was the last thing I heard before he turned off the radio.

"Y'all don't have nothing just like my house. Y'all ain't got the web, y'all ain't got Sega, y'all don't even have a CD player. Back home I had all that shit." Jarek said, reaching his long arms overhead and back over the couch.

"Well, my mom is crazy, you know that. She thinks technology is evil and now we're too broke. Even if she didn't hate that stuff, we still couldn't have it." Ethan said.

"She did order us a pizza, though, right?" Jarek asked.

"Nah, she said she left 10 bucks to go and get something ourselves." Ethan said.

"Man, this town don't have no place to eat." Jarek said.

"Maybe we should go into the city, get some food, rent a movie." Ethan said.

"Anything is better than this," Jarek said, getting off the couch.

We went upstairs, where Ethan instructed me to use the restroom. Grabbing our jackets, we started for the door when Ethan realized he forgot the money; he headed back into the house; Jarek and I waited outside. After a few minutes, we grew impatient and went back into the house.

"What's taking so long?" Jarek asked, calling out to Ethan.

He didn't answer, so Jarek and I started down the hall when Jarek shouted out, "Hello?"

"In here." Ethan's voice called out from Mom's room.

Jarek was looking through Mom's dresser, shuffling papers around.

"I can't find the money. She said she left." Ethan said.

"Well, I got some money." Jarek said.

"Let me check one more place." He said.

Ethan slid open the door of Mom's closet, rummaging through the top of Dad's old dresser, which Mom moved in there after he died. She kept all of Dad's things. I even remember the day he brought that dresser home from work; I was in preschool while he was still working on his PhD, so for money, he was employed at a furniture store. We had moved into a new 2-bedroom apartment, and I remember how happy Mom was that he could get such a good deal on furniture. We were on the second story with no elevator, so Dad carried it up the stairs piece by piece and re-assembled it.

"Found it." Ethan said, grabbing the 10-dollar bill, causing a business card to drop to the floor.

Picking it up, Jarek looked it over, then handed it to Ethan, asking, "What's this?"

Looking at the card, Ethan said, "It's Dr. Cody's business card. You know, my mom's boss."

"Didn't you say he used to work with your dad?" Jarek asked.

"Yeah, I suppose." Ethan said.

"What's the number on the back?" Jarek asked, grabbing the card out of Ethan's hand and turning it over.

"I don't know, it looks like a code." he said.

"A code to what?" Jarek asked, then looked like he had an idea.

"I dunno. Just put it back." Ethan said.

"Alright, let's eat." Jarek said, placing the card back on Mom's dresser.

Jarek still wanted pizza, so rather than going into the city, we headed for Gino's.

Tony whizzed by his waist length hair held in a fishnet as he hollered to the kitchen staff to, "Get off your ass."

"The orders are coming in faster than we can..." A voice was heard saying.

"No excuses in my kitchen. I never turn down an order." Tony said as he took an enormous ball of dough and rolled it on the table.

There were 4, maybe 5 white tables inside and a few outside, all of which were full of teens. The chatter was incessant, as each voice competed for my attention. I tried focusing on the blaring music, an angst filled hybrid of hard rock and punk, but was soon jarred from my meditation by the sound of a pile of broken dishes coming from the kitchen. Seeking refuge, I cupped my hands over my ears, but to no avail.

Ethan graciously took me outside to wait while Jarek went in to order. Standing on the perimeter of the outdoor dining area, I detected that Ethan's eyes were fixated. Peering in the general direction he was looking, I spotted two girls sitting across from one another, conversing. The one facing my direction wore a metal laden smile that bounced off the light. She was cute, petite, with a tomboyish look. Her hair was short except for her green streaked bangs that delicately fell over her right eye, causing her to brush it aside every few seconds. The green of her eyes matched her glow, as it did the tiny streak in her bangs. Her companion faced the other direction. Her straight spine, sturdy gate and broad shoulders gave little doubt that even though she was no more than 15, she already knew exactly who she was. The heat from our peering caused her to turn around as the restaurant doors opened, unleashing the sound of Green Day's "2000 Light Years Away" from their Kerplunk album (of course). The snappy punk love tune spoke of a boy with a crush on a girl way out of his league.

Snapping back in her chair and whipping around, she hoisted her white leather jacket, putting it on, one arm at a time, before walking towards us in slow motion (or that's how it felt to me). Her full, wavy dark hair held back with a headband, revealed her light brown eyes and olive-colored skin, while the tiny mole on her strong neckline peek-a-booed with her tank top.

She was bigger than her friend, not that she was chubby, not even a little, but taller, athletic, and strong, like a modern-day Athena. The beautiful blue glow emanating from her was matched only by her face.

"What's up peeping tom?" She asked, patting Ethan on his chest, causing her hair to whiz by my face, lingering the aroma of coconut.

Looking stoic, Ethan lifted his chin as if to say, 'What's up' back. Then Jarek approached with pizza box in hand.

"Hey Lucinda. What's going on tonight?" Jarek asked.

Lucinda? I thought it suited her.

"Not you. Who's your friend?" She asked, gesturing towards me.

"Oh, that's Ethan's bro. Who's that on your shirt? Your dad?" Jarek asked.

"Huh? What? No, that's George Carlin," she said, glancing down at her tank. "Oh my God, rude, does he have a name?"

"Michael." Ethan said.

"Hey Michael, you taking pity on these dorks?" She said, winking at me.

I reached my hand to her, and to my surprise, she walked around, linking arms with me.

"You're the sweetest," she said, as I put my head down, laughing shyly.

Her friend bobbed over, noticeably peering at Ethan, while her smile gleamed before quickly looking down.

"How's your friend?" Lucinda's companion asked.

"Oh, you mean Jason? I don't know, we heard he's back in the hospital. We were thinking about going over there. You guys want to come with us?" Jarek said.

"No, we can't. My mom is picking us up." Lucinda's friend shyly said.

"Looks like she's here right now." Lucinda said, gesturing to a blue Volvo pulling up.

Lucinda's friend smiled and waved as they both sauntered to the car and got in. Glaring, Jarek smacked Ethan's arm.

"What?" Ethan asked, irritated.

"You know what! Why didn't you say anything?" Jarek asked.

"What was I supposed to say?" Ethan asked, like he knew he was defeated.

"I don't know. 'Hi Samantha, I love you.'" Jarek said, giving Ethan another smack on the chest.

Hmm, Samantha? I wondered if this was the Sam I heard them talk about.

"Anyway, let's go," Ethan said, returning the smack on Jarek's arm as we left.

"I think we should still go to the hospital." Jarek said, pulling a slice of pizza out of the box and putting it in his mouth.

"Shit, hot," Jarek said, pulling the pizza out of his mouth. "Hey, who's George Carlin?"

Ethan shrugged in response; I didn't know either.

It was late when we arrived at the hospital. Handing Ethan the pizza box, Jarek stepped to the counter, though no one was there. Realizing visiting hours might be over, Jarek turned to us, silently placing his finger over his mouth as if to say 'quiet', then tiptoed around the counter, typing Jason Greene into the computer. Looking at us with a smirk, he headed out from around the counter when one of the nurses approached from the back.

"Hey, you. Can I help you?" The nurse asked as we dashed to the elevator.

"Pizza delivery!" Jarek said with a holler, as we furiously pressed the 'close door' button on the elevator before it shut on the nurse's face.

Chuckling, Jarek hit the button for the 5th floor, whereupon our arrival, Ethan and I started to get out.

"No, come back guys, I just did that to make her think we stopped at 5. Jason's on the 3rd. Floor." Jarek said.

Still chuckling, we got back on the elevator and headed to the 3rd floor.

When we arrived at Jason's room, he had a series of balloons tied to the edge of his bed post. They were an array of colors except the one in the middle that was a shaped like a toy truck. His shoulder length hair was shaved to a military cut, the kind with that tennis ball feel. He was staring off into the distance despite the television being on. When we walked into the room, he continued to stare without noticing our presence.

"Hey man." Jarek said.

When Jason didn't look up, Ethan said loudly, "Hey man, you here?"

"Oh, hey guys," Jason said, looking towards us finally.

"So how you feeling?" Jarek asked.

"I'm fine. They're treating me well here. It's better that I'm here. I wasn't ready to return home." Jason said.

"Yeah, okay. Sounds good, man." Jarek said.

"You want some pizza?" Ethan asked, pulling out our last slice from the box.

"No thank you, I've eaten." Jason said.

Jarek and Ethan glanced at one another. While Ethan shrugged his shoulders, Jarek returned with hands up as if to say, 'I don't know.'

Then the nurse who had followed us early entered the room.

"It's past visiting hours. You have to leave," she said.

"Okay, we're leaving." Ethan said, then reached his hand to touch Jason.

Jason returned his head to where it was when we entered and did not respond.

"Take it easy, man." Jarek said, but still no response.

Escorted out by the nurse, we stood in front of the hospital, where Ethan pulled out the last slice of pizza, placing it in his mouth.

"Anyone want the last slice?" Ethan asked with a mouth full.

"You do, obviously. How can you eat at a time like this?" Jarek asked.

"What do you mean? I didn't want to waste it." Ethan said, folding the empty pizza box in half and shoving it into a trash can.

Walking home, we were quiet for a while until Jarek broke the ice. "Man, this place keeps getting weirder and weirder. I was better off staying in South Central. Y'all need some Marshall law up in here, like we had during the riots. Figure some shit out. I mean, what do you think is going on with Jason?"

"He's been hacked by an evil element inside an evil hospital. That's doing evil experiments." Ethan said.

"You sound sarcastic, except it's true." Jarek said.

"I mean, all we've found so far is a crazy lady, a conspiracy rag, and a dude who works at a health food store, none of which can prove anything. It adds up to nothing. We have no connection to anything about my dad that is helpful. It probably was just a heart attack from years of smoking." Ethan said.

"That's bullshit and you know it. What about the CRO report? And the station wagon?" Jarek asked.

"Our paranoia, everything so far can be explained away by pure paranoia from a couple of kids who watch horror movies, play D&D and…" Ethan said, as he grew quiet, realizing we were already home.

With the house dark and empty, Ethan turned on the lights, heading downstairs. Jarek plopped on the couch with a sigh, while Ethan threw on "Siamese Dreams". Ushering in that iconic drum roll at the beginning of "Cherub Rock", followed by the guitar's urgency. It felt appropriate.

"I'll admit it's weird to see Jason like that. You know? The transformation, it's weird, he seems to be getting worse." Ethan said.

"We gotta do something," Jarek said.

"Do what?" Ethan asked.

"Figure it out," Jarek said.

"What?" Ethan asked.

"Oh, you gonna play stupid? Come on man, this, this place." Jarek said, looking and gesturing towards everything around him.

What alarmed me most about Jason's appearance was that his glow was gone. Most people carried the same glow as long as I knew them. On rare occasion someone might change like how Ethan changed from blue to red, when Dad died, but I have never seen one disappear completely.

Chapter 20

MOM'S MISSING?

After staying awake all night watching cult classics on Channel 9, we woke up around noon to the sound of the phone ringing. I heard it ringing several times before but was too tired to care, so I went back to sleep. After the third call, I could hear Ethan saunter down the hall and groggily answer.

"Hey," he said.

"Oh. Hi . . . uh . . . I don't know. Can you hang on?" Ethan said, as he placed the kitchen phone on the counter and walked into Mom's room.

Hearing this, I got up and followed Ethan. Jarek was still sleeping on our couch. Strangely, we found Mom was not in her room. There was no sign of her throughout the house.

"Yeah, she must be on her way because she's not here." Ethan told the person on the other line.

"Okay, sorry about that. I don't mind walking over there to pick her up. Oh, I appreciate that. Thanks so much." Ethan said.

Then, walking over to Jarek, he pulled off his blanket, slapping him on the foot.

"Hey, what?" Jarek said, snapping up.

"That was Laura's Mom." Ethan said.

"Who? What?" Jarek asked, still half asleep.

"The phone, it was Alyssa's friend Laura's mom." Ethan said.

"Oh, I didn't even hear the phone," Jarek said, rubbing his eyes.

"Dude, my mom was supposed to pick up Alyssa this morning and didn't show up, and she's not here." Ethan said, with distress.

"What the?" Jarek said with a puzzled look.

"What should I do?" Ethan asked, growing more distressed.

"Well, should we go get Alyssa?" Jarek asked in a calm tone.

"No, Laura's mom said that she can stay there another night. They were having so much fun that she was going to ask my mom if she could stay anyway. She was trying to catch her before she came over, but when she didn't show, she started to worry." Ethan said.

"Ahh, man, maybe she spent the night at a friend's house or something. Some moms party. It's no reason to panic." Jarek said.

"Okay, yeah, you're right... It's so unlike her to be irresponsible." Ethan said, trying to calm down.

I agreed. This wasn't like Mom at all. Some moms may stay out all night with friends and party, but not our mom. She's done nothing like that for as long as I can remember.

Having spent all our money the previous night on pizza, we rummaged through all the snacks in the fridge, trying to feed ourselves while waiting for Mom. As the day went by, we tried to hang out, listen to music and be normal, but there was an air of dread.

By night fall, I was hungry and worried; I began pressing my chin into Ethan's arm.

"Yeah, man, you're right," he said, then called out to Jarek. "Hey dude, this is getting weird. I need to do something."

"Yeah, I wasn't sure if I should say anything," Jarek said, walking over to where Ethan and I were standing in the kitchen.

"So, what should I do?" Ethan asked.

"Do you know any of her friend's numbers?" Jarek asked.

"No, I mean, she doesn't have that many friends. She used to when we lived in the city, but here, she just hangs out with us. I mean, I don't know. If she does, I don't know any of them." Ethan said.

"Okay, well, don't take this the wrong way, but we need to consider the possibility that..." Jarek said.

"That she was abducted by the man in the station wagon?" Ethan said, rolling his eyes.

"Dude, I don't know. Call the police then." Jarek said with a tinge of hostility.

"Don't you need to be missing for 24 hours?" Ethan asked.

"I don't know. Maybe that's just in the movies. Besides, it's been close to that, hasn't it?" Jarek asked.

Ethan took the phone and dialed 911.

"Hey, yeah. Hello, I am reporting someone might be missing . . . My mom . . . A little over a day, I think . . . She's old, 42 or something. She was going to a grief counseling thing. Yeah, we're fine. Okay, thank you." Ethan said to the operator, then hung up. "We have to wait."

"Wait? For how long?" Jarek asked.

"I don't know. She just said call back if she isn't home soon and they'll send over an officer." Ethan said.

He started into the living room, sitting on the couch with his hands on his head. He began rocking back and forth.

"This is so messed up," Ethan said, looking up at Jarek.

"Okay, man, it's alright. Let's get outta here," Jarek said.

"Where? Go where?" Ethan asked, interrupting.

"I have an idea but I'm not sure you're gonna like it." Jarek said.

"Oh no, we're not going to that place. That is crazy. They're bound to have cameras everywhere." Ethan said.

"Hear me out. Hear me out. First of all, those cameras never work. They had those all over LA to catch people doing whatever and they never worked, okay? Trust me on that." Jarek said.

"I would be incredibly stupid to trust you." Ethan said.

"Dude, no, okay. Well, what about Tony's friend? That David guy or that crazy lady, maybe she can help us," Jarek said.

"I wouldn't know where to find that David guy, Country Life is definitely closed, and Gino's is probably closed too." Ethan said.

Looking at me, Jarek went over and grabbed an alphabet board from his backpack, leaning up against the couch. Then, racing over to where I was standing, tapping on my toothbrush, he took the toothbrush out of my hand and placed the board in front of me.

"What do you think?" Jarek asked.

Flapping my hands, then walking around him in a circle, I had to think about what I wanted to do. It was a crazy idea, but I was feeling stir crazy waiting.

'L,E,T,S,' I spelled, as Jarek said, "Lets."

'G,O, F,O,R, I,T' I spelled as Jarek, without saying a word, looked over at Ethan, smirking.

"Alright, let's go," Ethan said.

Without hesitation, we got ready, took Dr. Cody's card with the code on the back and were off. Walking to Lizzy's house, there was a November chill, and, in our haste, Ethan forgot to bring my jacket.

Arriving there, it was dark. We knocked on the front door, the windows, then went around to the back where we had let ourselves in that one night to see if the door was open. It wasn't, so we banged and yelled to her to see if we could get any answer.

"Do you have her number?" Jarek asked.

"No, I gave her card to Mom." Ethan said.

"Alright, well, what do you want to do?" Jarek asked.

Without a word, Ethan started walking, and we followed.

"We'll go for it but if it goes all wrong, I'm blaming you guys." Ethan told us as we hastened our step and followed him to the big building.

Chapter 21

THE BREAK IN

When we got there, Jarek took Dr. Cody's card and typed in the code. The doors opened immediately. He grabbed the handle, and we walked inside.

Before leaving, we had each taken a flashlight to navigate our way around but hadn't turned them on until now, as it was ominously dark.

"Holy shit, I can't believe we're inside." Jarek said.

"Shh. What if someone's here?" Ethan asked.

"Where should we look? You know, for clues?" Jarek asked as we gingerly used our flashlights to look around.

"Any computer should do." Ethan said as he tried opening one of the office doors. Then, trying another, he continued, "These all seem locked."

"There, over there," Jarek said, pointing to the front reception desk.

Ethan sat in the receptionist's seat as Jarek and I stood around him. He turned on the computer and waited for the screen to come up. I had never heard a computer turning on before. Initially, it carried this, *err, ah . . . eh . . .* screeching noise followed by a slow, sustained buzz.

"It's locked." Ethan said, looking at Jarek.

"Well, let's figure it out." Jarek said.

"People usually use the names of their children, birthdates…" Ethan said.

"Or pets?" Jarek said as he picked up a picture of a poodle.

"How are we supposed to know the dog's name?" Ethan asked.

Jarek took his flashlight and shone it on the picture.

"It's got a tag, but I can't make it out. Maybe a C, something…" Jarek said.

"Think of a cutesy dog name beginning with a C." Ethan said.

"Cara, Cat, Cadence. Uhm, it looks a little like there's another C. Try CC." Jarek informed Ethan.

"CC? That's not even long enough. It needs to be four characters. How about Cha Cha? No. that's not it." Ethan said.

"Hmm, CC… Oh, there used to be a CeCe's pizza back home, spelled C-E-C-E. Try that." Jarek said.

"Boom. We're in." Ethan said with a smirk.

"Holy shit. Okay, so now what? What are we looking for?" Jarek asked.

"My mom already said there's nothing under my dad's name," Ethan said.

"What about Michael?" Jarek asked. Ethan looked at him with a puzzled face. "I mean, Lizzy knew him, right?"

"I guess. Couldn't hurt to try it." Ethan said. "No. Nothing. How do we connect the hospital to this place?"

"Hmm. What about Dr. Greene? You know, the brown man." Jarek said.

"Holy shit! There're tons of documents with a Dr. Greene." Pausing, Ethan sat back and took his hand to his face, then continued. "But just for a second here, I need to ask why we decided to break and enter a shady building that could have our balls? I mean, what the actual hell? Mom's missing, so how is this supposed to help?"

"Clues, man. If your mom being missing has something to do with her investigation into your dad, we need to build a case, you know? Help them find her, you know?" Jarek said.

"Alright," Ethan said, turning back to the screen.

"There are so many with Dr. Greene, I don't know where to begin." Ethan said.

"Can you cross check?" Jarek said.

"Yes, of course I can cross check it, but to what? I checked Michael, I checked my dad," Ethan said.

"Moms had me read this like 1000-page book when I was way too young to understand it," Jarek said.

"Your Mom sounds as crazy as ours." Ethan said.

"Man, y'all don't even know. Anyway, it was all about double speak." Jarek said.

"What's that?" Ethan asked.

"It's like when you say something but mean something else," Jarek said, then stopped, noticing the puzzled look on Ethan's face.

"There're words. You have these words that hide the truth. They're like codes." Jarek said.

"Okay, well, what double words should I check?" Ethan asked.

"It's double SPEAK, and I don't know," Jarek said.

"Hmm. Alright, let's think, it's all about the hospital and those experiments, right? So, it's going to be 'double speak' about that. It's going to have something to do with how their trials go wrong, Right?" Ethan said.

"Oh, damn. There was a part about that. The author said there was a surgery that went like horribly wrong. I think the guy was killed or something and they used these phrases to cover it up," Jarek said.

"What phrase?" Ethan said. "We don't have much time, the longer we're here…"

"Yeah, I know, give me a minute. I'm gonna try to remember." Jarek said while he looked as if trying to summon the thoughts from his brain.

"Therapeutic something, it was a … Therapeutic?" Jarek said, then continued looking up. "Therapeutic error? No, Therapeutic mishap? No, Therapeutic misadventure? Yeah, that's it! Try therapeutic misadventure."

Ethan typed the words into the computer, and we waited. Looking at the screen, Ethan's face lit up.

"Oh, man, we have therapeutic misadventures galore. It's almost all of Dr. Greene's. Hang on a minute, hang on a minute," Ethan said while moving closer to the screen as if to see it better.

"This one is about Jason," Ethan said.

"Jason?" Jarek asked.

"Jason Greene," Ethan said.

"Is there a way to print it out?" Jarek asked, looking around his shoulder.

"I'm sure there is, anyway, but I don't see a printer anywhere. Why are you looking around? Did you hear something?" Ethan asked.

"No, I just think we should bolt." Jarek said.

"Yeah, that sounds about right. I can't read this anyway. It's all Greek or Latin or something," Ethan said. "Let me check the settings to see if a printer… Yup, a printer is plugged in."

"It's gotta be attached to one of these cords." Jarek said, reaching behind the computer and tracing the cords to their prospective plugs. "Here. Turned it on, try it."

Once Ethan started printing the document, I noticed I needed to go to the bathroom. I ran off into the dark space when Jarek pulled up in front of me with his flashlight, giving me a start.

"Dude, we're almost done. Give us like five, maybe ten minutes to print this shit and we're outta here." Jarek said, taking my hand and bringing me back to the desk.

After what felt like much longer than ten minutes, Ethan said he had it and took the papers from the printer tray, folded them in a square and tucked it inside his jean jacket. Turning everything off, we couldn't wait to leave. The minute we were out of the building, Jarek and Ethan took off running while I stayed and relieved myself. Seeing they were half down the block, I tried breaking off the flow, but it kept coming. Realizing I was still in front of the building, Ethan started running back towards me; when I pulled up my pants and ran towards him, he stopped and waited. Off in the distance, Jarek was just crossing the street when the station wagon with tinted windows pulled up directly in front of him, almost hitting him. Jarek tried running when two large men sandwiched him, grabbing and throwing him in the car. While I continued running to Ethan, he had turned around to see the station wagon and started running back towards me. Speeding up, the car pulled up right next to him as the two men got out and started chasing him, then one of them grabbed him by the jean jacket and pulled him back.

"Michael, run away!" Ethan screamed as the second man came around and helped push him into the car.

Then the first man came towards me and when I froze, he took my hand, pulling me towards the car. Stiffening up, he was forced to stop as I sat on the ground.

"I'm not going to hurt you. I'm here to protect you." The Man said.

The car door opened, and I could see Lizzy leaning forward.

"Michael, you need to trust us," she said.

The man put his hand out to me as I took it, stood up, and entered the car.

Chapter 22

THE CRASH

The man shoved me into the back of the station wagon, where Jarek and Ethan were already sitting. Ethan took my hand, letting out a long deep breath at the sight of me. Lizzy sat across from us, looking very different in a black pantsuit, high heels and her hair held back tight. Our two abductors were up front.

"I'm sorry to be so dramatic, we were worried about you guys." Lizzy said.

"What's going on? Do you know where our mother is?" Ethan asked.

"I need to know what you guys were doing in the building." Lizzy said.

"Is our mom in danger?" Ethan asked.

"I'm not going to lie to you. She probably is in danger, but that's what we're trying to prevent." Lizzy said.

"Who are you?" Jarek asked.

"We work for interested parties." Lizzy said.

"Interested in what? What does that even mean?" Jarek asked.

"I can't get into details right now. What documents were you looking for and why?" Lizzy said.

"Where are we going?" Ethan asked.

"We're going to an undisclosed location." Lizzy said.

"This is just great," Jarek said.

The car approached a large open field when a gate opened automatically. The car drove into a building with a round roof, which looked like an airplane hangar. Getting out of the car, I could see that it was practically empty. The car, a few chairs, the two men, Lizzy, Jarek, Ethan, and I were all that was inside. Lizzy instructed us to sit in the chairs.

"It is quite serious, what you've done, and if I don't protect you, you and your mother could be in serious trouble. Do you understand?" Lizzy said.

"No, I don't," Ethan said.

"You can't just pull a gun on us on Halloween, then snatch us up off the street and not give us a clue." Jarek said.

"Yeah, who are you? Do you even own that herbal store?" Ethan asked.

"Yes, I was a nurse at the hospital," Lizzy said.

"Wait . . . are you the one who David was talking about?" Ethan asked, interrupting.

"What? David?" Lizzy asked.

"Oh yeah. You used to be a nurse at the hospital." Jarek said. "What about the station wagon? You said it was following you too."

One of the men came in, holding a briefcase. Inside the briefcase was a black clunky computer folded in half. He opened it and showed Lizzy the contents.

"We think we have found your mom's location." Lizzy said.

Standing up from my chair, I started flapping my hands while running back and forth. Grabbing Ethan by his jean jacket, I used all I could to pull him up, ripping his inside pocket, causing the document to fall out. One man reached down and took the papers still folded in a square off the floor. Opening it, he held it up and handed it to Lizzy.

"We'll review it in the car. Let's move." Lizzy said.

The man pushed me to move faster and shut the door, knocking me hard on the forehead. I sat down, wincing and rubbing my head as I could feel the bump forming. A slow whining cry started coming out of me.

"You, okay?" Ethan asked, reaching over and taking my hand.

"How do you know where Mrs. Hogan is?" Jarek asked Lizzy as she intently read the document.

"I... We've been trailing you. The other side probably is too." Lizzy said.

"What other side?" Ethan asked, beginning to shout.

"You guys like CIA or something?" Jarek asked.

"Or something. I'll explain it all when there's time. Right now, I am trying to save your mom's life." Lizzy said.

"You think her life's in danger?" Ethan asked, with a quiver in his voice.

"I hope not." Lizzy said, looking up briefly.

"What about Jason? Is he okay?" Jarek asked.

"Jason's your friend?" Lizzy asked as her voice softened.

Looking over at Ethan and me, then back at Lizzy, Jarek nodded.

"They don't usually use subject's real names, so it probably isn't him." Lizzy said.

"It says Jason Greene, that's his name, exactly his name. What are the odds it isn't him?" Jarek said.

Lizzy stared down at the document, ignoring Jarek's question.

"But why?" Ethan asked.

"Genetic information. Similar studies have been conducted on rats to see which genes are switched on and off. It holds potential for surgeries and/or medicines to help those with epilepsy or other neurological conditions. It stands to make any drug-maker billions, plus it's another step to further 'perfecting' humanity." Lizzy said with air quotes.

"They're experimenting on people without their consent, including minors and causing these . . . misadventures. How are they getting away with it?" Ethan asked.

"If we have anything to say about it, they won't anymore. They have a lot of pull and we're not sure where they're getting it. We need documents like these to build a case, but unlike you fellows and whistle blowers . . ." Lizzy said, trailing off.

"If you guys are such bad asses, tracking people and what not, then why do you need us?" Jarek asked, throwing his hands up.

"We are held to certain standards; we need to go through certain legal avenues to get into the building and their computers." Lizzy said.

"Are you guys with the government? Aren't those the bad guys?" Jarek asked.

"Sort of. It gets complicated. Certain factions of the department will have a . . . difference in philosophical views, let's say." Lizzy said.

"Is Mom a whistle blower? Was Dad?" Ethan asked.

Lizzy looked up as if in her brain, looking for the right lie or consoling information, or at least trying to remember. Then the car slowed down as the man in the passenger seat turned around and told us to 'hush'. The backseat of the station wagon was cramped, but I tried rocking back and forth, while flicking my fingers in my face anyway.

"Oh shit! GO! IT'S A TRAP!" The man in the passenger seat yelled as the driver started speeding up.

Lunging forward, we were nailed by a large white van pushing us sideways. Ethan reached his hand over my head, tucking it down, covering it with his arms as we plunged further into chaos. Then we stopped moving. The two men in the front got out, as we could hear fighting. Ethan let go of me when I looked over to see Jarek and Lizzy passed out. Ethan smacked Jarek in the arm and face several times, urging him to wake up. When he started opening his eyes, I breathed a vast sigh of relief.

Flinging the door open, one man yelled, "GET OUT! GET OUT! RUN!"

Ethan took me by the hand and yanked me out of the car with more strength than I knew he had. Jarek, now fully awake, tried waking Lizzy to no avail.

The man yelled again, "NOW!"

As Jarek pushed me from behind, we got out and started running. Though I didn't dare turn back to look, I could hear the men engaged in a brawl. My urge to stop and plop to the floor was thwarted by Jarek's constant pushing and Ethan's constant pulling, as they forced me to move faster than I would have thought possible. In the night's darkness, it was near impossible to know where we were, so we kept running. At one point, Ethan took hold of my shirt and pulled me down to the ground, instructing me to keep still and quiet. Jarek took his lead while all three of us smashed to the ground, which felt of dried itchy grass, and hid under a rusted-out hood from one of those classic ca rs.

I don't know how I did it, but I remained calm. My insides were terrified and the bonk on my head was pulsating but, on the outside, I stayed still and silent. The fragrance of motor oil and garbage wafted through the air as the wind picked up, and I shivered from the cold. Noticing my lack of coverage, Ethan inched closer, smooshing himself into me, trying to keep me warm. Picking up on the cue, Jarek did the same on the other side, altering my state from freezing to barely manageable. We could hear the men from outside the car hood as they searched for us. Their flashlights were visible as they lurked around, searching. Were these the good guys or the bad guys? How could we know the difference? Without answers to these questions, we remained put. I prayed to God, Grandpa, Dad and whoever else might be listening to let us make it through this. The men could be heard arguing about which direction we went when there was a loud clatter, sounding of banging metal or garbage cans being turned over coming from several yards in the distance. Following the sound, I heard their footsteps moving away from us as I finally breathed, sank into my dry, itchy bed of weeds and tried to fall asleep.

Chapter 23

THE ABANDONED BUILDING

The next morning, I was awakened by the faint sound of scratching on the car hood. A couple of coyotes were searching for their last meal before heading to bed as the sun rose. I wiggled around, trying to break free from the wedge I was in between Ethan and Jarek. Ethan woke up, giving me the gesture to remain quiet and stay put as he slid out of our shelter. In his absence, the brisk air wisped around my exposed arms once again, reminding me of my lack of covering. Needing to go bad, I wiggled my way out from under the hood to find Ethan taking a whiz as I joined him. With Jarek still sleeping, Ethan reached under the hood, giving him a couple of whacks to wake him.

Looking around, Ethan took stock of our location. "It looks like a junkyard."

Lifting his arms above his head and letting out a long yawn, Jarek asked, "Now what?"

"I don't know. We need to check in at home, see if Mom's back, check in with Alyssa, and then go to the police, not necessarily in that order." Ethan said.

Ethan started walking so we followed. The junkyard was huge, and we couldn't make heads or tails of how to get out. Exhausted, I tried several times to sit down, only to have Ethan or Jarek pull me up and let me know in no uncertain terms that there wasn't time for rest.

"Over there!" Jarek said, pointing toward a broken fence that led to the street.

He headed towards it, then crouched down to get through while Ethan started pushing me from behind and ducking my head so I could get through as well.

Abruptly, a tall, thin man grabbed Jarek from around the corner and put his hand over his mouth.

Ethan cried out, "No Michael!" As he tried pulling me back through the fence, causing my pants to snag on one of the exposed chains ripping them open, leaving a painful gash in my thigh.

Two men appearing from nowhere, clubbed us both over the head. Groggy but still awake, what felt like a bee sting on my neck, followed by the sensation of a cold liquid entering underneath my skin, caused my legs to buckle and without even knowing how I got there, I was o ut.

The next thing I remember was waking up not in my own bed. My eyes opened, then closed again, struggling to stay alert while trying to remove the haze. A slow hum buzzed in my ears, then quieted in a rush, bringing awareness to my screaming headache. There was a draft as I lay cold on the concrete floor. Nothing was working. My limbs, my head, my fingers, and toes were heavy so that any attempt to move resulted in my falling back. Having no idea who, why or where I was, I tried scanning the room. It appeared hazy, like I was looking through a camera with a smudged lens.

Once the fog began to clear, the first thing I noticed was a white utility van, looking exaggerated like a puffy, bouncy castle. Behind it was a large garage door, next to a small red door, and near that a fire extinguisher case. Then I saw someone I believed to be the thin, tall man sitting on the edge of a desk. Two figures across the room were lying asleep on the floor. Thinking they were likely Ethan and Jarek, I immediately got up, but my balance was off, and I wobbled, nearly falling. The thin man came towards me. He was speaking, but all I could hear was a buzzing.

In one rush, the sound returned, and I could hear the thin man say, "Whoa, whoa, whoa, watch yourself."

Continuing my drunken walk, falling again, the thin man caught me. The clanking sound of the key ring attached to his belt loop let me know that my hearing had returned as he dragged me across the warehouse room, planting me alongside Ethan. Nudging Ethan, I was able to wake him up. He looked groggy, but managed to look over at me. I got up again and started pulling Ethan's arm to get him up when I noticed his hands were cuffed behind his back.

Approaching me, the thin man said, "Whoa, there fellow, don't get crazy."

Yanking me over while pressing me into a chair, he then tried handcuffing me, but I resisted. Pulling away while grabbing the sleeve of his jacket, I attempted to pull him down, but he was able to restrain me and locked me to the chair. I violently tried releasing my hands from the cuffs, causing a hot rush to overcome me as my breath became shallow. I struggled to bang my head on the chair, but the back rest was too short. Leaving me no options, I screamed and cried loudly while tears rolled down my cheeks.

A woman in a suit with matching heels, short curly hair, and a brown glow came clacketing over and instructed the thin man to un-cuff me.

"Please, I can't stand it. He can't do anything. That's the retard." She said.

Once un-cuffed, I ran to Ethan, sitting next to him, grabbing his arm while digging my chin into it. Returning to consciousness, he looked at me with worry. I was comforted by the fact that he was awake but further frightened by the fear on his face.

"What can we do to calm him down?" She asked Ethan.

"Give him something to bop," Ethan said.

"Bop?" The thin man asked.

"Uhm. Like a pen or a ball or a cup." Ethan said.

The woman took a water cup and handed it to me. I drank the water, then started bopping the cup.

"Also, music might help." Ethan said.

"That'll do." The woman said.

'Ah, music', I thought to myself, raising my head up, swaying from side to side, as I started singing "Today" by The Pumpkins.

Da da Dada den na na na, da da Dada den na na na,

The thin man and two other brown, glowing goons stood behind the woman while she took a chair and sat in front of us. She looked back at one of the men behind her, gesturing towards us. The man took a water bottle, pouring it on Jarek's head, who was still asleep lying near Ethan.

"So, which one of you has been stealing highly sensitive documents and providing them to a Ms. Kara Barton aka Mrs. Laura Barton aka Ms. Hazel Barton aka Ms. Hazel Henderson aka Ms. Elizabeth Kinney?" The woman asked.

We remained silent, so she spoke again. "Hello? You mute too? Which one of you has been stealing stuff and giving it to that lying witch?"

Coming to, Jarek lifted his head and asked, "You mean Lizzy?"

"Sure, Lizzy. Why not? You're the son of a Major General, are you not?" The woman asked Jarek.

"What? No, my dad's dead. You mean Gramps?" Jarek said.

"Oh right. So why would you want to involve yourself with Lizzy?" The woman asked.

"We hardly know her," Jarek said when Ethan leaned over and gave him a look.

"Why are you asking us about her? We don't even know her," Ethan asked.

"Well, she knows you. She has been tracking you, bugging your phones, your house, your car..." The woman said.

"How do you know that?" Jarek asked.

"Son, I really don't want to hurt you, but if you interrupt me again," she said. "We know because we've been following her."

"We don't know anything. We've been..." Jarek said.

"You were at the building last night. What were you doing there?" She asked, interrupting.

The room stayed silent as no one said anything for a few minutes.

"Okay, if you don't want to tell us what you were doing or what you saw, then we'll have to give you a little motivation." She said, gesturing to the thin man.

The thin man walked over to Ethan, forcing him to stand, aggressively shaking him. I started to get up when Jarek took his foot, launched it over me, using it to keep me down.

"Please don't hurt my mom or my brother. We really don't know Lizzy. We met her a couple of times. We accidentally ended up at her house on Halloween." Ethan said.

"You think that was an accident? No, Ms. Lizzy, as you call her, is all calculated. She set you up to go there so she could entice you into stealing documents for her. She doesn't have the balls to go in and steal them herself because she knows if she did, we'd nail her ass. She doesn't have anything on your dad." The woman said.

"What about Michael?" Jarek asked.

"Who's Michael?" She asked.

"Him." He said while gesturing towards me with his chin.

"Oh, total fabrication. She doesn't have anything on him. All of it was bullshit to get you to spy for her. The station wagon. She led you to her house. You are the victim of a pathological sociopath who wants to win at all costs. We've been watching it all unfold." She said.

"If we're the victim, why do you have us tied up? We don't know anything, whatever we had we gave to Lizzy. Let us go. Please." Ethan said.

"I'd love to, but I'm under strict orders." She said.

"Orders from who?" Jarek asked.

One of the goons dragged Ethan over, standing him in front of us. Getting up again, Jarek took his leg and tried to push me back down, but I broke free and darted to Ethan. Flapping on his handcuffs, I tried pulling his hands out. The thin man smacked my hands, then started moving him towards the van, while one of the goons came over and whispered something to the woman. Both goons and the woman walked through the red door, disappearing. I continued to follow Ethan as he wiggled, making it difficult for the thin man to move him.

Oddly, in this moment, I thought about Jason, remembering one afternoon on Kite-Hill he had his boom-box. Right in the middle of Nirvana's "Smells Like Teen Spirit", he stops the tape.

"I love my boys, but I'm getting sick of this shit. How about you?' He asked, turning towards me.

Truthfully, I don't know if I could ever get sick of that song, but he pulled out the tape, tossed it into his backpack, and grabbed another.

"This is what started it all, the grandfather of hard rock. That's all this grunge stuff is hard rock, you know?" He asked, his back still turned to me crouched down as he jammed the tape in the boom-box.

He rewound without stopping first, making that horrible mouse squealing noise. Not the greatest start, but I was eager to see where he was going with this.

"You'll see what I mean, grandfather. Check it out," he said, standing up while placing his hand on my shoulder, banging his head to Motorhead's "Ace of Spades".

"Ahh, shit, here it is. This is my TRACK, man," he said, in response to the lightening paced music, then jumping up and into me.

"Hey what are doing, man?" Ethan asked.

"Just a little slam dance, dude. Never hurt anyone," Jason said, while slamming into Ethan, then everyone else.

The fellas started grumbling and I could hear a faint, "Dude, this isn't a show."

Undefeated, Jason sauntered over to me laughing, turning up the music, then put his hand on my shoulder.

"That's me man, 'The Ace of Spades', like Lemmy, you know? I can't let it get me down, you just gotta live while you can take a chance. We all end up with 'The Ace of Spades', you know?" Jason said, to my bewilderment.

"Hey, I know Lemmy is God and all, but can you put on something in this decade?" Jarek said.

Ignoring Jarek, Jason continued, "You're a sweet kid, but tough, you know? You're Michael, Michael the archangel. He takes the wicked and blasts them back to the Lake of Fire... You look like you have no idea what I'm talking about."

"Yoouuu gonna let him corrruupt your brother like that?" Darnel asked Ethan.

"It just means we learn from you, man. Not the other way around and don't let anyone tell you any different," he said, ignoring their hazing.

Taking matters into his own hands, Jarek pops in a tape. The melody starts strong, familiar, like I'd heard it on the radio.

"Ah, man, why you gotta do me like that?" Jason asked Jarek, then paused for a moment recognizing the song.

"This is a great tune, actually. This is a good one for you, man. Listen to the lyrics. Everyone tells you it's in the trees, the skies, the ground, society... You know, other people. No, it's not, it's in you, just find your desire. It's in you, man. It's in YOU. You feel me?" Jason said, placing one hand on my shoulder and patting the other on my chest.

Previously flapping, I went still, feeling steady, calm, and confident. For the remainder of the song, we stood quietly, listening.

Back in the present, the song from that day (which I later found out was Ned's Atomic Dustbin "Grey Cell Green"), played in my head.

Watching Ethan being shoved into a van, a surge of adrenaline coursed through me, when I completely forgot the multiple lumps on my head, the blood dripping down my leg and the near-death experience we were facing. I bounded over to where he was, my feet heavy on the ground, and summoned the strength to push the thin man with enough force to knock him over.

Lying on the floor, he glared up at me in shock, as I scrunched my eyes shut, defensively pulling my forearms over my face while thinking, 'holy crap, what did I just do?'. Hearing the woman's voice, I opened my eyes to see her standing in the doorway, gesturing to the thin man who was an inch from destroying me.

"What are you doing? Leave them be, they're not going anywhere, get over here," she said, summoning the thin man.

Giving me one final death stare, he followed her orders, and they made their way through the red door.

"Damn, you just tossed that dude," Jarek said, as I realized we were alone in the warehouse.

"Michael. Hey, Michael, I need you to grab those keys off the floor." Ethan said, using his foot to gesture to the ground where my push had apparently knocked the thin man's keys off his belt loop.

I knew what he wanted me to do. I saw the shiny metal resting on the ground, but my body wouldn't listen, so rather than grabbing the keys, I walked to Ethan, yanking his arm downward. Wobbling, he caught his barring, making his way to the keys as he crouched to pick them up from behind with his arrested hands.

"Hey Michael, help me up, man," Jarek said as I went over to lift him.

Attempting to unlock himself, Ethan dropped the keys, "Shit, Michael. You need to help. I need you to get the keys."

This time I was able to pick up the keys, but while attempting to place them in Ethan's hand, I dropped them once again to the floor.

"Shit, Michael. Please, I need you to focus. If we don't get out of here, we're dead. You need to get those keys and unlock me." Ethan said.

I picked up the keys once more and by this time, Jarek had made his way over to us.

"Hand 'em to me," Jarek said, holding his shackled hand out.

With the keys firmly in Jarek's hand, he made his way over to Ethan as they stood back-to-back while Jarek attempted to un-cuff Ethan.

Fumbling through each key, Jarek announced, "Yes, I got it. This is it."

Free now, Ethan used the keys to un-cuff Jarek. Then they both ran to me as Ethan grabbed me by the shirt and started pulling me towards the door. Frozen, I stood stiff, unable to initiate my body to move.

"Dude for real? Now? Think of Mom, Alyssa. We got to get the frick outta here!" Ethan said.

I started to loosen allowing Ethan to pull me as we noticed Jarek making his way to the fire extinguisher, pulling the lever, breaking the glass, then taking the device.

"What's that for?" Ethan asked.

"A weapon." Jarek said. As the red door flings open, the thin man and one of the goons bounds through the doorway.

Jarek sprays them with whatever is inside those extinguishers, buying us some time as Ethan leads us through the grey door, to the outside. I take off running when I realize Ethan and Jarek are standing in front of the door. Ethan holding the nob while Jarek searches through the keys to see which one will lock the door. I run towards them when I see Jarek has locked the door.

"Go, GO..." Ethan shouted, running while the garage doors to the warehouse begin to slowly raise.

Unexpectedly a rusted 1970s VW van speeding our way, stops in front me. The door slides open, revealing David crouching in the back.

"Come on!" He screams as we all leap into the vehicle.

With the garage door out of sight, I can only imagine that soon there will be a utility van following, but looking back, I see nothing.

"What the hell, guys?" David asked.

"It's all true, man, it's all true." Jarek said.

"You guys, okay?" Tony asked, who I realized was driving the van.

"I had a feeling you guys were in trouble, then I saw you running," David said.

"And by 'had a feeling' you mean, 'I happened to be buying my weed in the area'," Tony said.

"Well, whatever. You guys look messed up. We should get you to the hospital." David said.

"NO!" Jarek and Ethan said in unison.

"The sheriff's department. We need to report a kidnapping." Ethan said.

Chapter 24

THE SHERIFF'S DEPARTMENT

On the way to the sheriff's office. Jarek explained to David and Tony what happened.

"Holy shit, man. You guys are in it. I mean, you're in it DEEP. This is wild." David said.

"Are you sure the woman in the car was Liz?" Tony asked, glancing back before putting his eyes back on the road.

"Pretty friggin' sure." Ethan said.

"Dude, I told you about her," David said.

"You told me shit. And I'm still not convinced it was her." Tony said.

"What if she's working with her ex? Maybe they're back together," David said.

"Would you shut up?" Tony said as he pulled in front of the sheriff's department. We all started to get out when David put his hand out, blocking us.

"Wait, wait, wait. I . . . uhm . . ." David said.

"What? Let them out." Tony said.

"But what about the stuff?" David asked.

"Your weed? They're not going to search the car." Tony said. "Okay, fine, I'll take them inside and you drive the van back to the shop."

"No, no, I want to talk to the sheriff too." David said.

"Fine, I'll take it back to the shop and pick you guys up later. Okay?" Tony said.

"Okay, but make sure it's all gone," David said, as he barely shut the van door before Tony buzzed off. "He's so uptight," he continued, patting our backs as we headed into the building.

Upon entering, a young, attractive blonde woman in uniform stood up from her chair and walked over to the counter.

"What do you think you're doing here?" She asked David with a knowing smile.

"I'm here to see you, my love." David said, taking her hand and kissing it.

"You stop it," she said, pulling away with a smile, swatting his arm.

"Is he in?" David asked.

"No, it's the weekend, and he doesn't want to talk to you, that's for sure," she said.

"You may need to call him in, this is big." David said.

"What now? Alien invasion or something?" She said, laughing.

"Uh, no, nothing like that," David said, turning towards us.

"What's with the kids?" She asked.

Then a colossal figure of 6'5" with dark hair and olive skin bounded through the door with a gust. "Ah, speak of the devil." David said, turning to him.

"I don't have time for you today," he said, walking past without looking, then headed to the counter. "There's been a break in at the big building, some kids it looks like."

'Oh shit', I thought, so much for the broken cameras Jarek mentioned. Looking at Ethan and Jarek, they had the same expression as the thought running through my head. Desperately wanting to leave, I began pulling on Ethan's sleeve.

"Who are you?" The massive figure asked.

"They have a crime to report, a kidnapping. It's some serious shit, man." David said.

"And who are you, their babysitter?" The man asked.

Before David could respond, he continues, "You kids need to come with me."

Walking to an interrogation room, he directed us to sit on one side of a table as he remained standing on the other. Pouring coffee into a Styrofoam cup, he shuts the door revealing a sheriff's hat hanging on the back, which he placed on his head, covering his black slicked back hair. He then opens the top of a metal drawer, pulling out a sheriff's badge and placing it on his belt buckle, hanging over his jeans.

"I received a call at home on my day off. Said three teenage boys broke into the big building last night, whole thing caught on camera. Now what are the chances that when I see that tape, I'm going to see you three boys on it?" The sheriff asked.

No one answered as the tension got to me, causing me to abruptly stand walking towards the door. "Hey, ho, what's going on here?" He said, stretching his arm out in front of me blocking my path. I took his arm and dug my chin into it. 'Wah, wah, wah,', I said.

"Wait a minute, fella," he said, then turning to Ethan and Jarek. "Which one of you is responsible?"

"I am," Ethan said, lifting his hand. "That's my brother. We were digging around the building because I was worried about my mom. She works there."

"If you're worried about your mom, why didn't you call us?" The sheriff asked, as I released his arm.

He directed me to go back and sit down, then handed me a cup of water, which I chugged before bopping.

"He did. Y'all said to call back later." Jarek said.

"Well then, why didn't you call back later? You're hanging around with that crack pot over there," he said, gesturing towards the door. "And he'll get you thinking there're all kinds of shit going on–medical experiments, genetic altering, and soul snatching. Did he put you up to this?"

"No, we were just looking for my mom. I still don't know where she is. She was supposed to come home two nights ago." Ethan said.

"Well, why'd you come in here? Were you turning yourself in? Because if you were, that may go better for you," Sherriff said.

A knock on the door was followed by the young, attractive blonde entering.

"There's a Dr. Kinney here." She said as a man wearing a dark grey suit slumped in behind her.

"Yeah, so? I'm conducting an interrogation. Tell him to buzz off," The sheriff said, looking right at the man.

"I'm sorry to interrupt Sheriff, I am with Special Forces," he said, flashing his wallet open, showing the inside.

"With all due respect, that means shit," The sheriff said.

"I need to speak to the boys." Dr. Kinney said, gesturing towards us.

"I don't give a shit. I need to speak with the boys right now so you can take them in on your time, in your jurisdiction. This is mine." The sheriff said.

The attractive blonde deputy leans over, tapping the sheriff on the shoulder. He bends down, allowing her to whisper something in his ear.

"You got to be kidding me. Okay, you have 5 minutes and I'll be on the other side of that window watching, so no bullshit," The sheriff said. He walked out, closing the door behind him. Dr. Kinney entered and sat across from us.

"Hello, gentlemen, Ethan, Jarek, and you must be Michael," he said.

"Who are you?" Ethan asked. "What the hell is going on?"

Dr. Kinney leaned in close, like he was about to tell us a secret, when I noticed his glow was yellow. His hair was mostly brown with a little grey and his skin was pale except for the black circles under his eyes. Despite this, he was a decent-looking guy, old and tired, maybe in his late 30s.

"That's a good question." he said.

"Friggin' A," Jarek said.

"Friggin A is right. What were you guys doing at AmeriGen?" He asked.

"What the hell is AmeriGen?" Ethan asked.

"The big building." Jarek said.

"How do you know that?" Ethan asked.

"How do you NOT know that? It's in all those articles from the New Liberator." Jarek said.

"I never paid attention to that," Ethan said.

"Boys, please," Dr. Kinney said.

"Dude, your mom works there," Jarek said.

"SHUT UP. Please," Dr. Kinney said.

"We already said we were looking for my mom." Ethan said.

"Your mom is fine. She's at your sister's friend's house," he said.

"Who? Laura?" Ethan asked.

"I suppose. She's fine, that's all you need to know. She's probably home now, wondering where you are," he said.

"Wait a minute… Kinney. Dr. Kinney. Isn't Lizzy's name Kinney?" Jarek asked.

"Yes, that's my wife." Dr. Kinney said.

"Wife or ex-wife?" Jarek asked.

Lifting his eyebrows, glaring at Jarek, he said, "Ex."

"Is she okay?" Jarek asked.

"Yeah, she's injured, but okay. She'll recover. I'm here to inform you that we are very appreciative of your work handing over that document to Mrs. Kinney. It was helpful information from what I've heard; though it was not recovered." He said.

"Can someone please tell us what's going on?" Ethan asked.

"Yes, of course. Mrs. Kinney and I work for certain factions in the government," he said.

"Yeah, we heard that part. What the hell does that mean?" Ethan asked.

"It means we're trying to help you. We understand what happened with your father and-" he said.

"You know what happened to my father?" Ethan asked.

"We have our theories, though it can't be proven at present," he said.

"All that shit in the Liberator is true, I told y'all! That shit is true, right? Right?" Jarek asked.

"I don't know about that. All we're concerned with is protecting individuals from partaking in non-consensual activity; which is what we're afraid is happening with respect to AmeriGen and their relationship with the local hospital," he said.

"And by 'activity', you mean experiments?" Jarek asked.

"Something like that," he said.

"Well, who was that, knocked us over the head, injected us with something, then took us to that empty warehouse, nearly killing us?" Ethan asked.

"That wasn't one of ours," he said.

"Who are they, then?" Ethan asked.

"We believe they are another division of our department that has the opposite agenda." he said.

"It's like the Cold War, remember?" Jarek said. "The American spies pretend to be Russians spying on Russians, then become Russians for real and spying on Americans, while Russian spies do the same in reverse, right?"

"Sure," he said, looking at his watch, then over at the window where the sheriff said he'd be. "Look, I need you boys to pay attention here. You can't do anymore poking around AmeriGen or looking into your dad. If you keep it up, I mean this investigation of yours. I can't promise that we can protect you."

"Protect us? Where were you when we were knocked over the head, drugged and dragged into an abandoned warehouse? You didn't protect us, we got out ourselves—" Ethan said.

"Look, you little shit," he said, getting heated. "I mean, if you don't keep it-"

The door aggressively flung open when the sheriff bounded through.

"Times up." The sheriff said.

Dr. Kinney stood and started for the door, where another man in a suit was waiting for him.

"But we still don't know what the hell is going on," Ethan said.

"Just know that we are here to help. You and your family should be fine. We'll be sure of it." Dr. Kinney said.

"What about me?" Jarek asked.

"You too. Oh, and fellas, be sure to keep it," Dr. Kinney said, pushing his hand towards the ground as if to tell us to 'keep it on the down low', then proceeded to swiftly walk out.

The sheriff stood in the doorway, making sure that Dr. Kinney and his companion had left, then slammed it shut.

"Creepy government shit for brains," The sheriff said under his breath, watching the men leave through the window.

"Alright, it's your lucky day. I received a call that your tape has gone missing, and the big building has no evidence, therefore is dropping all charges." The sheriff said.

"For real? Ah shit, finally something good." Jarek said, resting his head on the table.

"Watch your language, young man. Now, get outta here, but stay away from that place and stay away from that douchebag, patchouli-smelling hippie." The sheriff said.

"It's not patchouli," Jarek whispered into Ethan's ear as we walked out.

"What's that?" The sheriff asked.

"Nothing. I mean, yes sir." Jarek said.

It all felt so unresolved. We were walking out of there like we were the ones getting off easy when there were actual bad guys trying to hurt people. We were safe if Dr. Kinney was to be believed, but what about the people on the 13th floor? What about the little girl? What about Dad? I started grabbing Jarek by the arm, which I had never done before.

"Hey what's up?" He asked.

"What are you guys doing here?" A female voice asked in our direction. When I looked up, I saw it was Lucinda. The Green Day song "2000-Light Years Away" that played that evening at Gino's when we met popped into my head.

"A misunderstanding. What about you?" Ethan asked.

"My dad works here," she said, gesturing towards the sheriff.

"That's your dad?" Jarek asked in astonishment.

Lucinda gives a look to Jarek as if to say, "Yeah, stupid," then turns to me as I dig my chin into Jarek's arm once more.

"Are you okay?" Lucinda asked, running to my side.

"He's had a helluva day." Ethan said, coming over as I kept digging into Jarek.

Once I saw Ethan close, I stopped digging into Jarek and went to aggressively grab Ethan, to which he grabbed back.

"Hey, hey, what's going on?" The sheriff asked, separating us.

"Maybe he needs to say something," Jarek said.

"Now isn't the time." Ethan said as I lunged for him again. The sheriff blocks me, grabbing my arms and putting them behind my back.

"Daddy, stop. He's the sweetest. He doesn't mean it." Lucinda said, coming to my side, trying to pull her dad's hands off me.

"Does anyone have an alphabet board or chart?" Jarek asked.

Everyone went silent as they looked around in confusion.

"Alright, how about a piece of paper and a pen? Please?" Jarek said, as the young blonde deputy came over and handed him what he asked for.

Jarek took the pen and wrote the letters of the alphabet as boldly as he could on the piece of paper, then approached me, holding it in front of me.

"Sir, I need you to let him go. So, he can talk," Jarek said.

"Daddy, please." Lucinda said.

Then the sheriff released me as I stood flapping with nervous stage fright.

"It's okay." Lucinda said, calmly steadying my hand.

Looking at her, the song came to mind again and would each time I saw her from that day forward.

I spelled, 'S, T, then S, T again,'

"We don't have time for this..." The sheriff said.

"Daddy, shut up," Lucinda said, then gestured for me to continue.

'T,H,E,R,E, I,S, A, G,I,R,L,' I spelled then Jarek, taking away the paper, said it out loud, "There is a girl. What girl?"

'T,H,I,R,T,E,E,N,T,H, F,L,O,O,R', I spelled as Jarek took the paper away again.

"13TH. Floor. He's talking about the hospital. The 13th floor." Jarek said.

"The 13th floor is for authorized staff only; you can't get up there." The sheriff said.

"No, he did. We were there that night. There was a power outage and somehow he ended up there." Ethan said.

"Go on, Michael." Lucinda said, gesturing to Jarek to hold the paper up for me again. 'S,H,E, I,S, B,E,I,N,G, H,U,R,T' I spelled then started to make typos, 'S,T,U...'

"All I got is 'She is being hurt.' That's it." Jarek said.

"Does this have anything to do with that greasy government slime ball here a minute ago?" The sheriff asked.

"I believe so, sir." Jarek said.

"Daddy, you have to see if something is going on. You have to go to the hospital and investigate." Lucinda said.

"I don't have anything to go on," The sheriff said.

"He just said," Lucinda said as the front door opened and in walked Mom and Alyssa.

"Oh my God! You're here. What in the world is going on?" Mom said, racing over, giving me a hug while Alyssa wrapped her arms around my legs.

"Mom, where were you?" Ethan asked, running to her as she turned to hug him.

"I was at my conference in Denver, just like I told you," Mom said.

"What conference?" Ethan asked.

"You know, I said, Dr. Cody wanted me to go in his place because he was staying with his brother and…" Mom said.

"Oh, right," Ethan said with a look of recognition. "So, you didn't go to your grief support group that night? But what about Laura's Mom calling and saying you didn't return to pick her up the next day?"

"The crappy car broke down on the freeway as I was heading back. I tried calling you, but the machine didn't pick up and there was no answer. I called the Johnsons' house, and they came and got me. When I got home, you guys weren't there. At first, I figured you were at Jarek's, but when I called his house," Mom said.

"You called my house?" Jarek asked.

"No one answered. Anyway, after a while I got worried, and the Johnsons were nice enough to drive us here. So, what are you guys doing here?" Mom said.

"They were worried about you. Apparently, you guys got your wires crossed." The sheriff said as we all looked at him in shock. "I got a tee time that started 10 minutes ago."

Chapter 25

CHRISTMAS 1993

Over the next several weeks, we did as Dr. Kinney instructed, (even though he was a jerk) and kept everything that happened to ourselves. It was terrifying and to think that we may have put our family in danger was the worst part. So, we told no one, not even Mom. If she knew, she would probably force us to tell the sheriff or, even worse, leave Jukeville. I knew we weren't supposed to be doing any more digging but, in my heart, I felt if we left, we'd never discover the truth about Dad, which I was secretly determined to do.

It was December and Christmas was upon us once more. Unlike last year, the Hallmark card was a little less dazzling. The twinkle walking down Main Street was a lot dimmer as everything reminded me of Dad. I thought about the many Christmas tree lighting ceremonies in San Francisco I spent on Dad's shoulders while the fake snow rained down, wet and cold. Here the snow was real and while the streets aligned with pure Christmas magic, there was an ache, an emptiness that remained the entire holiday season.

I wondered if everyone else felt this way too until Christmas morning, when I knew for sure they did. The tree stood beautifully adorned with all our home and school made ornaments from Christmases past.

Alyssa ran to the bottom of the tree, pulling out each box, reading the label, then looked off into the distance, staring at the ceramic stocking I painted in first grade. I could see that even as shiny and bright a soul as she was, she felt the emptiness. Mom knelt beside Alyssa and held her close. As they embraced, a silence filled the house with no words spoken, only the sound of A Christmas Story playing on the T.V. in the background.

Breaking the ice, Ethan lifted a present wrapped in newspaper and held together with small strips of black electrical tape, then shoved it into my stomach. Winded from the blow and a little confused, I let the gift drop to the ground.

Picking it up and handing it back to me, Ethan said, "Go ahead, it's for you, dummy."

Holding the gift, I looked it over and knew I wanted to open it, but didn't know where to begin. I picked at it, then held it to my face, bopping it, but it was heavier than I expected.

"Oh, I'll help him, let me," Alyssa said, heading over to me on the couch, pawing at the gift.

Tearing through it, within seconds, Alyssa revealed a scratched up old 1980s Sony Walkman, complete with headset. Elated and laughing, I lifted my fingers to my face, giving my nose a tickle.

"Try it out. It's got batteries and everything." Ethan said, taking it from Alyssa and putting the headphones around my head.

"When'd you get that?" Mom asked, wiping the tears from her cheek, smiling.

"A guy from school got a new one, sold me his old one. It's from me and Jarek." Ethan said, then pressed play.

The tape crackled, then the tail end of U2's "Acrobat" faded as the background melodic tune picked up. Once I heard the unmistakable voice, I knew it was The Pumpkins' song, "Drown".

Every stance reminded me of Dad. I knew it was probably about a girl, but there was a longing, a distance that couldn't forsake his love. That longing was strong this Christmas Day.

Holding the case, I got off the couch and circled the living room when thoughts of the town swam through my head. Like a hawk, I glided through Main Street, where the lights looked brighter than before. The people clutching their packages smiled and laughed, while the oversized Christmas tree in the middle of the square stood erect, appearing majestic but warm. I saw the houses with their decorations adorning their snow-covered lawns.

I sailed over Jason's enormous, cold museum of a house, where no one was home, then past Lucinda's where through the window I witnessed the sheriff wearing an ugly Christmas sweater and dozens of children playing; driving the adults crazy.

Finally, leading up to our own front door, where the entire family, including Dad, stood outside, building Alyssa's snowman clan.

Funny thing was, it wasn't a memory or a dream. Oddly, it felt like a vision.

As the song ended, I looked around, hoping someone would come over and help me rewind, when I realized most of the presents had already been unwrapped. Alyssa squeezed a white fluffy stuffed cat, which she called 'Kitty-meow-meow', while Ethan sat leisurely back on the couch, sketching in his new oversized artist pad.

Before I knew it, Mom tapped me on the shoulder, causing me to drop my Walkman, disconnecting it from the headset.

"Don't break it already, dick," Ethan said.

"Hey, language sir, it's Christmas." Mom said as Ethan buried his head back into his sketchpad. Picking up the Walkman, Mom took the headphones off my ears, plugged it in, taking a listen.

"See, it's fine," she said, taking the headset off and placing the device down on the dining room table.

"This one is for you too, sweetie." Mom said, handing me a gift wrapped beautifully in red with a gold bow.

Holding it, Mom came around and pulled on the bow, then gestured for me to do the same as I untied it. Turning it around, she gestured for me to pull off the tape, then gently pulled the rest of the paper back. I liked the sound of the ripping paper, wanting to hear more. I ripped again, though the paper was completely off already.

"Honey, here," Mom said, handing me the contents, which was a book, *The Adventures of Huckleberry Finn*.

Pealing back the hardcover, I read the inscription which simple stated, 'From Santa', smiling I reached for Mom giving a long hug.

Despite everything, it turned out to be an alright Christmas. At dinner, we sat around the dining table for the first time since Dad, holding hands as Mom said grace. Once the peripheral of my eye caught the sight of my Walkman resting on the cabinet, I drifted off thinking of that scene of all of us on the lawn making snowmen.

Chapter 26

SIAMESE DREAMS

A few days after Christmas, the ice-skating rink was hosting a winter break party to raise funds for the local schools.

"Mom, this is going to be awesome! Laura is taking lessons, I really want to take lessons," Alyssa said as Mom parked Dad's old jalopy.

"Shut it," Ethan said.

"Why? Why do I have to shut it? You're being rude," Alyssa said.

"Okay, everyone shut it. We're here, so get out." Mom said.

"What about lessons, Mom?" Alyssa asked, stepping out of the car.

"I can't afford it right now. I barely got the car fixed. I'm paying for the AM/PM club. That's all I can handle right now," Mom said.

"It's okay, Mom. I don't need lessons." Alyssa said, hugging Mom around the waist.

"Thanks, sweetie." Mom said.

"Ugh. I hate this place already." Ethan said, rolling his eyes as we walked towards the entrance.

Inside, the impressing cold felt like a weight around my face, neck, and hands. I liked the feeling and stood flicking, trying in vain to capture the sight of my breath. The rink was filled with students and their instructors as the party goers waited for their turn. Classical music piped in from the rickety old speakers that hung from the ceiling on opposite ends of the room. Through my peripheral, I noticed several pieces of lint on the outside of Mom's sweater, causing me to lean and pick them one by one.

"Thanks, honey," Mom said, turning to me with a smile.

Abruptly, I was shaken by a change in music that had a pounding drum and guitar riff. I could recognize it even in my dreams. The Smashing Pumpkins' "Geek USA" came pounding through the speakers, causing the skaters and on-lookers alike to whip their heads around trying to find the culprit. "Who changed the music?" Some lady asked.

Then, I saw her. Like a Christmas angel, Lucinda glided on the ice with a regal stance.

Speeding past, causing a gust, she barreled through the others, practically pushing them aside, like she was the only one on the ice. The other skaters huffed and scattered while she leapt and spun with a quickness that made it look easy, though I knew I could barely stand on the ice, even with a walker.

Before long, she was alone. Even the instructors stood aghast around the oval-shaped arena. I anticipated the songs change in tempo, where everyone in the rink disappeared into a ring cloud. Lucinda didn't miss a beat, gracefully slowing along with the pace of the song.

As the song spoke of a dream, I saw myself gliding alongside her, holding hands, then merging at the wrist, like a pair of Siamese twin skaters, lovingly looking back at one another.

The morose turn in the song brought in a black, ominous cloud like the ones you see before a thunderstorm. Then the brown man,

Dr. Greene, appeared. Without warning, he is there on the ice with Lucinda and me, but it's me he wants.

Taking me by my free hand, I pulled away, though his grip was strong. He yanked hard while Lucinda cried out, but no sound came from her lips. The black cloud turned to a blood red, as his yank caused our wrist to pull apart.

Once the sound returned to white hot speed, I broke from my trance hearing the rushing of the crowd as now everyone, including the once forlorn skaters, are cheering for Lucinda when she stopped, reluctantly smiling at the crowd's enthusiasm.

On the move once again, she slowly glided past with both feet facing in the opposite direction, leaning as if she was casually up against a wall. Catching my eye, she flashed a smile, then winked, instinctively causing my head to turn down as I laughed, flicking my fingers in my face

.

Breathing heavily, Lucinda pulls off another rare smile then curtseys to her roaring audience. The loudspeaker announces, "It's now time for free skate," causing the crowd to rush in and Lucinda to exit.

"Wow, she was great, don't you think?" Mom said, placing her hand on my shoulder, giving me a shock. "Oh, I didn't mean to startle you."

"Hey," Lucinda said in front of me.

"Hello, you were great." Mom said.

"Thanks so much." Lucinda said graciously.

"Oh my God, you were like, amazing out there. I'd love to skate like that," Alyssa said, racing to Lucinda, giving a hug.

"Aren't you sweet? You should take lessons, ask for my class." Lucinda said.

"Ah, no, that's okay, I can't," Alyssa said.

"Uh, yeah, we'd love to, but it's not in our budget right now." Mom said.

"No, no charge, I mean, it's the Lucinda scholarship." Lucinda said, leaning down to Alyssa's level. "Don't tell anyone though, okay? Just show up on Saturday morning at 10am. Sound good?"

"No really, that's not necessary," Mom said.

"Hey, it's fine. I don't mind, really. Just don't sue if she sprains her ankle and we should be good." Lucinda said.

"That's way too nice of you," Mom said.

"It's no problem, I'm friends with your son." Lucinda said.

"Oh, you're friends with Ethan. I think he's around here some-where." Mom said, scanning the rink, noticing Ethan sitting on the bench flirting with Sam, the green-haired girl from the pizza place.

"Who? Oh, Ethan. No, I mean, Michael." Lucinda said, smiling in my direction.

"Oh. Yes, of course." Mom said, glancing over at me.

"I gotta go. I'm working today. I just wanted to say 'hi,' let me know if you need anything." Lucinda said, walking into the sea of people, out of my sight.

"Did she mean it, Mommy? I really get to take lessons with her?" Alyssa asked, tugging on Mom's shirt.

"Yes, I believe she did. We'll find out for sure on Saturday. Will you do me a favor, honey, and go get Ethan? Tell him I need to talk to him." Mom said, pointing at Ethan.

Alyssa ran over to Ethan, interrupting his game. He looked over at Mom, irritated, then got up and came towards us.

"What's up?" Ethan asked.

"I forgot to have Michael use the bathroom before we left. Can you take him while I go get the skates?" Mom said.

"Fine," Ethan said, taking me by the hand directing me to the bathroom.

After we came out of the bathroom, Ethan looked around for Mom, then spotting her, he took my hand and led me across crowds of people where I felt anxious and stopped.

"Oh, don't you do that to me here," he said, pulling my sleeve though I remained still. "I swear to God, you are killing me, dude."

Ethan tugged harder as I pulled away stronger, then reached forward, digging my fingers into his arm.

"Hey, just the two I want to talk to," the sheriff said, standing above us placing his hands on each of our shoulders. "Let's pop a squat. What do you say?"

Something about his domineering manner caused me to feel okay, and I started moving while he led us to an open table sitting across from us.

"Where's the other one?" the sheriff asked.

"Who?" Ethan asked.

"The other one, your third musketeer or whatever?" the sheriff said.

"Oh, you mean, Jarek? He's in California. Hasn't come back yet." Ethan said.

"Alright well you can pass this message on to him when he gets back as I don't care to repeat it," he said, pausing, giving a gigantic then scratching the 5 o'clock shadow around his chin. "Well. Very much against my better judgment, at the stubbornly strong urging of my daughter, I investigated the claim you made at the office that day."

"Which claim was that?" Ethan asked.

"You know, the spelling thing. Can you try to keep up here?" the sheriff said, still scratching his chin.

"Oh, right, yeah, sorry," Ethan said.

"Anyway. We went to the hospital; 13th floor and all. There was a girl there. She was, well, I don't need to get into all the details, but she wasn't being treated well. Not as far as I'm concerned, anyway. Let me just say we found her, and she has been returned to her grandmother, who has been looking for her for months." the sheriff said.

"Wait. What? You mean the girl Michael was talking about was real?" Ethan asked.

"She IS real. She's been safely returned to the custody of her grandmother." the sheriff said.

"Well, what happened? What were they doing to her? Is someone going to jail?" Ethan asked.

"I can't tell you the details. She's a minor and has rights. All I can tell you is her parents were not well and agreed to . . . uh . . ." the sheriff said.

"Sell her to science?" Ethan asked.

"They weren't well." the sheriff said.

"So, is someone going to jail?" Ethan asked.

"No, unfortunately what they did was considered 'legal' as they were given permission by the parents, who were believed to be fit at the time. But it wasn't received well by the hospital or the creeps at the big building and the doctor in charge has since resigned." the sheriff said.

"Doctor in charge? Dr. Greene?" Ethan asked.

"I can't confirm that." the sheriff said.

"Whoa, this is crazy. So, how did you-" Ethan said, leaning back in shock.

"Yeah, I'm done answering questions." the sheriff said, then looking over at me, sizing me up. "So, how'd you... you know? Figure it out? Figure out the spelling stuff?"

"Oh, it was Jarek. He noticed Michael one day when we were hanging in the basement, over by the alphabet board and-" Ethan said.

"No, forget it. I'm not that interested. Anyway, my daughter is pretty fond of you," the sheriff said.

"She is?" Ethan asked.

"Not you. Anyway, whatever you fellas were doing that day, you uncovered something, which I suppose was a good thing. But you know, don't pull that shit again," the sheriff said, standing up, looking around in either direction, then back at us. "You know, Sam is Lucinda's best friend. They grew up together, and she's like a daughter to me, so don't be a prick."

"No, I, uh..." Ethan said.

Briefly looking at Ethan, Sheriff gave the *shh* gesture with his hand then walked out of sight.

Chapter 27

SABOTAGE

On New Year's Eve, Mom said Alyssa and I could stay up 'til midnight. Alyssa got so jacked that she started blasting those noise makers, jumping up and down on the couch before passing out at approximately 10:14pm. For the remainder of 1993, she slept quietly, straddled across Mom's lap while we watched Dick Clark's Rockin' Eve. When the ball dropped, Mom took Alyssa to bed, then came back and waited for Ethan, who was supposed to be home no later than 1am. At the ice-skating rink, he managed to lasso a date with Sam. I couldn't wait to hear about it.

Around 1:23am Ethan arrived. Mom sat still, like she hadn't been anxious about him being late.

"How was your night?" She asked.

"Alright, I guess," he said, heading to his room.

"Happy New Year!" Mom shouted into the hallway.

"Yup, New Year." Ethan said, before slamming the door behind him.

"Urgh. Teenagers." Mom said, looking over at me on the couch. "Present company excluded."

She said nothing about Ethan being late and tucked me into bed.

"Happy New Year, honey. I'm glad I got to stay home with you these few days. I need to return to work on the 2nd. We'll start that new book of yours tomorrow and then we'll discuss it, okay?" She said, kissing me on the forward, brushing my hair aside.

I knew she was thinking about Dad, feeling guilty or something. She put on a brave face, but sometimes at night I'd hear her cry through the walls. I thought she must feel sorrowful that she couldn't stay home with us or worried that we had to grow up too fast. I didn't want her to feel that, but we all must go through whatever it is we have to go through. The holidays were tough.

New Year's Day was a Saturday and Mom had to return to work on Monday, but we didn't have school until Wednesday. Jarek was expected to fly home late Monday night, so we expected him to come by Tuesday.

When he arrived that afternoon, Ethan was still asleep. Alyssa and I greeted him at the door.

"What's up y'all?" Jarek asked.

"Whoa, I almost didn't recognize you." Alyssa said.

"You like it?" Jarek asked.

"I guess," Alyssa said with a shrug. "Let me wake up Ethan."

"You mean his lazy ass still asleep?" Jarek asked as Alyssa ran down the hall to Ethan's room. "What's up, man?" Jarek said, patting me on the back, guiding me into the living room.

I could hear Ethan bumble off his bed with feet slapping hard on the floor. He walked into the bathroom, and took a pee with the door open, then headed to the living room.

"Holy shit! What happened to you?" Ethan asked at the sight of Jarek.

"It's a new look. What do you think?" Jarek asked.

"It's different," he said, gliding his hand over the mohawk atop Jarek's head, then sliding his fingers on either of the bald sides.

"Y'all just jealous." Jarek said.

"No, it's good, just takes a little getting used to. It's cool, though." Ethan said, plopping on the couch, settling in while sizing up Jarek.

It was funny to see Jarek this way, as he was always so clean cut. Ethan and I took a cue from Dad and never gave a care about fashion. Our old wrinkled, hand-me-down t-shirts with shorts and sandals, even in the rain, contrasted the flawless polos with pressed khakis, perfectly un-scuffed high-tops that Jarek sported. And now here he was mohawk with red tips, torn jeans, Black Flag t-shirt, army jacket and combat boots. I sat next to him and tapped on the thick black studded band he wore around his wrist.

"Oh, you like that? Hollywood, baby," he said.

"And what's with the guitar?" Ethan asked, remarking on the guitar case strapped across Jarek's chest.

"Oh, shit, that's my axe!" He said, unzipping it from the case and pulling it out.

"Ah, it's sweet. Can I see?" Ethan asked, reaching his hands out.

"Yeah, let me show you what I learned." Jarek said, playing the opening of "Smells Like Teen Spirit."

"What's that?" Ethan asked.

"You don't recognize it? It's Nirvana," he said, playing it again.

"Oh, alright. Let me check it out." Ethan said.

"I told you my uncle is in the music business, right?" Jarek asked, handing the electric guitar to Ethan.

"Yeah, I think so. What's he do?" Ethan asked, strumming the axe.

"He listens to demos, then tells producers who to sign and shit. I got the latest Beastie Boys track right here, not even released yet," he said, patting his chest pocket. "He has his own band, too. He plays everything drums, bass, guitar. He taught me a few songs."

"He gave you this?" Ethan asked, still focused on the guitar.

"Yeah, it used to be his. He has a bunch of them. It was a bitch getting on the plane." Jarek said.

"Well, hey, I got some news too." Ethan said, stretching his neck out running his fingers down it.

"What's that?" Jarek asked.

"Can't you see?" Ethan asked.

"See? What am I looking at?" Jarek asked, then paused, looking more intently. "Do you have chicken pox or something?"

"No, dude, it's a hickey." Ethan said.

"Who'd you get a hickey from?" Jarek asked.

"Who'd you think?" Ethan asked.

"Oh, shit, no you didn't. You made out with Sam?" Jarek asked.

"We had a date on New Year's Eve. That's why it's faded. It was much bigger before. I had to wear my hoodie, like this," he said, gesturing like he was lifting his shirt over his neck.

"Ah, man, you must have finally talked to her then. When did that happen?" Jarek asked.

"I asked her out at the winter break fundraiser." Ethan said.

"Where was that?" Jarek asked.

"The skating rink." Ethan said.

"Oh, so Lucinda was there?" Jarek asked.

"Yeah, but she was working. Oh shit, I need to tell you something." Ethan said.

"Now what?" Jarek asked.

"Lucinda's dad, you know, the sheriff? Well, he came up to Michael and me at the skating rink and told us that they investigated what Michael said that day." Ethan said.

"No, they didn't," Jarek said.

"Apparently, they did, and guess what? He was right," Ethan said, smacking me in the arm. "There was a girl on the 13th floor being messed with and the doctor involved was fired."

"No way! Are you kidding me? I told you! Didn't I tell you? Who was the doctor?" Jarek asked.

"The brown man. You know, Jason's dad." Ethan said with a knowing look.

"No friggin' way. Ah man, I wonder if Jason's okay. Have you talked to him?" Jarek asked.

"What? No, I mean, what am I supposed to say to him? I don't think he knows it was us that got his dad fired, or I guess he wasn't fired but had to resign in disgrace." Ethan said.

"That's even worse. Sheriff told you all this?" Jarek asked.

"Yeah, me and Michael." Ethan said.

"Did you tell anyone?" Jarek asked.

"What do you think?" Ethan said.

"Not your mom, Sam? No one?" Jarek asked.

"Definitely not my mom. She'd lose her shit, and we'd have to move." Ethan said.

"Damn. Well, what was going on with the girl?" Jarek asked.

"That he wouldn't tell us. Privacy laws as she's a minor and all, but she's been returned to her grandmother." Ethan said.

"Dude, I mean, we got to see if Jason's okay," Jarek said, then sat back as if he was thinking of what to say. "See if he's okay, but without letting on that we're the ones who got his dad fired or resigned or whatever."

"Well, I don't know how we're gonna do that." Ethan said, putting the guitar on the floor and sitting up. "Hey, throw on that Beastie Boys demo. No one's heard it yet, right?"

"Yeah, we get to be one of the first. Where should I play it?" Jarek asked, getting up, looking around, noticing the boom-box in the living room, "Can I use this?"

"Yeah man. Whatever." Ethan said.

While Jarek squatted in front of the boom-box, a violent BOOM was heard, followed by the sound of shattering glass. Ethan and I pulled back like the time we see *Jaws 3-D* and the teeth were heading straight for us.

"What the hell, man?" Jarek asked, coming up behind Ethan, tip-toeing amidst the shard glass while I stood on the other side, laughing anxiously.

"I don't know," Ethan said, lifting a brick out of the rubble, plucking off a box taped to the other side, and causing the contents to fall to the floor.

I could see there was a ring, a pair of glasses, and a note. Ethan took the note and the ring while Jarek lifted the glasses.

"What is this?" Jarek asked, examining the glasses which were cracked.

"No way. No, this can't be." Ethan said, examining the ring in his hand.

"What?" Jarek asked, but I knew what Ethan was about to say.

"It looks like my dad's wedding ring." Ethan said, holding it to the light.

"What's the note say?" Jarek asked, swiftly snatching it from his hands, reading it. "You're closer than you think?"

Jarek studied the document made of cut out newspaper clippings reading 'YOU'RE CLOSER THAN YOU THINK', then handed it back to Ethan.

Speechless, we stood silent when Alyssa came bounding from her room.

"What was that?" She asked.

The Beastie Boys' "Sabotage" from Jarek's tape floated up and through us with a harrowing scream, as we stood in disbelief.

So many thoughts raced through my head, I lost track of all space and time. Was it a prank? Was it a message? If so, from who? And why? A cool wind came through the broken window, brushing my hair back as I sank deeper into the song.

I recall little of what happened later that day.

Acknowledgments

I have to start by thanking my husband, Ayron, for being patient, taking care of the kids, and bringing me food while I was working.

A very special acknowledgement must go to my 3 children, Avery, Aydan, and Alyce, for being the coolest people in the world and inspiring the characters.

A special shout out to my friends JMF, Virstyne Henry, and my mom, Bobbie Anderson for planting the seed, reading the early drafts and helping me edit.

A very special thanks to Pat Notaro, D.M. Gaivin, and the Handleys for being instrumental in helping Aydan find his voice.

And finally, I am eternally grateful to the spellers who so eloquently described their experience. Aydan Boden, Jamie Handley, Ido Kedar, Elizabeth Bonker, Naoki Higashida, all the cast of *Spellers* and so many more have taught me so much.

About Author

April Boden is a wife and homeschooling mom of 3 who one day decided to wake at 6am, go to a coffee shoppe, and start writing books. She eventually gave up the 6am wake-up calls and instead swapped T .V. watching for writing. In between educating, shuttling, and feeding her kids, she occasionally does housework and goes out to dinner with her husband. She lives with her family in Southern California.